CHARLIE'S SECRET

MELODY LAW

Charlie's Secret

Melody Law

ISBN 978-1-7367267-0-9

This book is dedicated to victims and survivors of domestic abuse. We all have a story to tell. Shamelessly revealing mine to set others free.

In loving memory of Esther Elaine Law

CONTENTS

FOREWORD

As a survivor of a 25-year long narcissistic abusive marriage, I am passionate about helping victims identify and escape these relationships as well as get the necessary help they need to heal.

Admittedly, I am still in the process of healing, and might be for the rest of my life; you may be too, and there's nothing wrong with that.

So, what is Narcissistic Personality Disorder (NPD)?

According to Psychology Today, "Narcissism is characterized by a grandiose sense of self-importance, a lack of empathy for others, a need for excessive admiration, and the belief one is unique and deserving of special treatment."

These are people who are so self-absorbed,

manipulative, verbally abusive, and feed off of attention. They don't care about you or anyone else and will go to any extreme to get what they want. The only reason they want you around is to keep receiving what you provide them whether it be finances, attention, or emotional vulnerability they can feed off of.

A narcissist will belittle you, exaggerate their achievements, monopolize conversations, fantasize about being powerful in any capacity, expect excessive admiration, feel superior, and behave in an arrogant manner.

Such people don't take criticism or opposition well. They respond with anger, rage, physical or verbal attacks, or any form of punishment as long as it negatively affects you due to not being agreeable to their actions.

Narcissists are neither reasonable nor do they take accountability for their actions. A narcissist will play mind games to deflect responsibility because they are obsessed with being viewed as perfect.

Recent studies have shown, being in a relationship with someone who possesses NPD can cause great emotional trauma that often results in Post Traumatic Stress Disorder (PTSD), anxiety, depression, memory loss, financial ruin, hypochondria and sometimes suicide.

If you are still in a relationship with a narcissist, I pray you find the courage to get out. You are worth more than being someone's emotional punching bag.

I hope my story helps you as much as it has freed me.

PREFACE

"Ma! Ma! He's tryna kill me!"

My son's loud, distressed voice jostled me out of my deep sleep. I jumped out of bed disoriented. I thought I was hearing things until my son called out to me again, but this time with a blood-curdling scream.

I sprang right to action and ran towards the direction of his voice. My bare feet slid around on the wooden floors that were freshly waxed the day before as I hastily made my way down the long dim catwalk hallway, highlighting flashes of lightning piercing through the two-story windowpanes.

My mind was racing with all sorts of terrible possibilities as I approached the split staircase, but none matched the sight before me when I descended the stairs. My soon to be ex-husband, Mark, was straddling our youngest son Junior choking him with one arm around his neck and the other forcefully pinning his arms together. Mark stood 6'3 in stature and weighed 310 pounds. While identical in height, Junior weighed only 160 pounds. It was like watching an alligator kill its prey with the death roll. I didn't know what had led to this, neither did I care. My sole focus was saving my son's life.

"Nigga you gone' die tonight!" Mark gritted his teeth menacingly. He had a deranged look on his face which terrified me because although I had seen that look many times before, this time it was worse and I knew first-hand what he was capable of.

"Stop!" I yelled with every breath in me as I pulled Mark's shirt, trying to help Junior break free. "Mark, you're hurting him! You're gonna kill him! Stop! Stop!" I screamed in horror.

I launched myself into their tussle with all I had and grabbed onto any part of Mark I could and used all my might, helped by my adrenaline rush, to push him off Junior, who then took this opportunity and ran for his life.

Mark's extra-large hands gripped my shoulders and lifted me off my feet and threw me to the side, out of his view, with so much force the wind was knocked out of me once I hit the floor. He ran past me, after Junior, yelling obscenities along the way. I got up wincing, and pursued him, hoping and praying my son had gotten to safety. Unfortunately, Junior was headed for the garage, which meant the only way out was into the torrential rain and thunderstorm.

I gathered all my strength and caught up with Mark, "God damn it... Stop!" I yelled again hoping he'd respond to the firmness in my tone of voice, but my efforts once again proved futile. My voice was now strained and cracking as I continued to yell in exhaustion, "Mark, please stop! Don't hurt him! I'm begging you! That is your son, Mark."

I stretched out my hand to stabilize my balance in the doorway while Mark was shoving me out of his way. I continued to plead with Mark to prevent him from bounding into the garage and battering Junior further... and that's when it happened.

To loosen my death grip on the doorway, Mark slammed the door repeatedly onto my wrist over and over until a loud crack reverberated through the room. Mark's head snapped in my direction, meaning he'd heard it too. That's when my world stopped.....

A pulsating heat flowed from my head to my

arm. I couldn't believe what had just happened... and then I felt the pain. Living with Mark for 25 years had taught me the true meaning of pain, and yet nothing could compare to the mind-numbing, excruciating pain I felt that day. The bone didn't break the skin, but I knew it was broken. My hand swelled immediately, and my eyes went out of focus as I felt the pain as a loud, throbbing pulse in my head.

"Bitch, look what *you* did! *You* hurt your mother!" Mark accused Junior for what he had done to me. Mark yelled more threats at our son who had hesitated at the garage door. Unfortunately, Junior had seen his father's double-mindedness and decided to save his life the best way possible. He pulled open the garage door and ran off into the night, completely vulnerable to the violent thunderstorm.

I had always made excuses for Mark. I had been living a lie hoping the perfect family everyone saw out in public would one day become my reality in private. But that night as I crouched to the kitchen floor in pain, my husband hesitated between taking me to the hospital and finishing what he had started with our son. Who on earth was this man I married?

I was married to a malignant narcissist. All the

signs were there. Everything aligned, but deep down inside I wanted it to work. Having come from an abusive home, I knew for certain that this wasn't the kind of life I wanted for my children or myself. In hindsight, staying only created more damage than I could have imagined. If only I had loved myself enough to walk away.

In actuality, nothing about my marriage made sense. There was no such thing as the honeymoon phase for us, but that was never a big deal because of my personality. Everything I had been through in life had caused me to become stoic, for lack of a better word, because I had both witnessed and been through too much. Being reserved when it came to almost every matter was my method of self-preservation.

Laying on that gurney in the Emergency Room after that incident was devastating in more ways than one. The doctors had to reset my wrist while I was awake. The pain was so intense I begged the doctors, nurses, anyone really, who would listen, to put me out of my misery.

I couldn't help but wonder where my son was and if he was okay. As a mother, I will always do everything in my power to protect my children, but that night I felt like I hadn't done enough.

Do you know that one of the effects of dealing

with a narcissist is that you make excuses for them? This was my unfortunate reality. When the police came to question me about what had happened, I told them I had fallen down the stairs. Yes, I lied to the police.

Honestly, my first instinct was to protect my family. I had high hopes by lying to the police, I was restoring peace in my family. I thought Mark would feel remorse at the very least. But narcissists are neither reasonable, nor do they take accountability for their actions, and I learned that the hard way.

1

LOVE BOMBED

With trembling hands and black mascara running down my face, dissolved by my salty tears, I pulled out my fuchsia Fenty lipstick and wrote on my bathroom mirror. The light was on, but the room appeared dark. My vision was clouded by an overwhelming feeling of despair.

What is real? What is the truth? Who am I?

"Charlie... lives... here," I softly read out the words I wrote on the mirror.

"Charlie... lives... here," I repeated, hoping my level of conviction would rise with the sound of my voice.

I could no longer distinguish between reality and my imagination. My reality had been manipulated for many years until all that remained was a shell of who I used to be. My mind and emotions were continually attacked by a man I called my husband for over 25 years, but how did it all begin? And why did it take me so long to figure out that something was wrong?

It all started in 1994 when my toddler needed his first haircut. I was a young, single mother living in a tiny apartment while studying and working full-time to make ends meet. My sole focus was on providing for my son to the best of my ability.

As a product of two hardworking parents, I learned how to be responsible at a very young age. My parents were workaholics who spent the majority of their time managing their multiple businesses. One thing I commend them for, though, is that they taught my sister and me the value of hard work. They were very successful entrepreneurs in Washington, DC, owning a gas station, liquor store, and a used car lot, so they split their time among these businesses.

Although I grew up in the inner city because my parents wanted to live closer to their businesses, I went to a Catholic school, so it sheltered me from the urban world around me and the fact I spent a lot of time alone at home. Unlike other kids, I could not go out and play on the street because my parents wanted to make sure I was safe, so I stayed indoors and admired the games and laughter I could hear going on outside.

Even though my upbringing was a lonely one, being a single, teenage mother was never a part of my life plan. I always dreamed of becoming a doctor someday. Just the thought of wearing a white coat would get me giddy, so I worked hard in school with this goal in mind. However, once I had my baby boy, my dreams took a backseat and he became my entire world. There was a sense of belonging and contentment when I had him I never felt before, and I thought that was all I needed in life, well, until I met Mark.

A charming, well-spoken, tall, and handsome man with chocolate skin. Mark was a guy with a magnetic personality any woman would easily fall for because he was such a smooth talker, always dressed to the nines and smelled captivating. He was one of those guys who could say complete nonsense, but people would still eat it up because he was a mesmerizing storyteller.

I was smitten by Mark, and the feeling caught me completely off guard. I was not looking for a relationship, neither was I eager to bring another person into my life after what happened to my boyfriend Eric. In the short time we were together,

Eric took on the role of a father figure to my son. He got us an apartment and took care of me far beyond what I needed or asked. Eric's family embraced my son and me as their own. They were loving and supportive, much to my surprise, and treated me as though I had always been a member of the family. As someone who came from an abusive home and lived a solitary life, the only person I ever had to rely on was me, so being around people who genuinely loved and supported me was not only refreshing but terrifying because I didn't want to lose that... but I did when Eric was killed.

His death shook me to my core. Eric had been my rock. He was proof kind people existed in the world and love didn't have to have any strings attached. It was while I was grieving the loss of Eric I met Mark.

I will never forget walking into the barbershop that day for my son's first haircut. Mark was sweet, funny, gentle, and had my son laughing infectiously in the barber chair. I would be lying if I said my heart wasn't moved by how gentle Mark was with my son.

"All done," Mark said, and fist-bumped Nathan. "Now that's how a man's supposed to look."

"Thanks, it looks good," I smiled kindly. "How much do I owe you?"

"Don't worry about it, it's on me," Mark replied with a charming smile.

Even though I was a single mother working hard to take care of my child, I wasn't one to jump at the opportunity for free things because I learned while growing up nothing was ever really free. I eyed Mark suspiciously as he dusted the chair and swept up the hair from the floor. He seemed like a nice guy, but then again, he was too nice.

"I'd rather pay what I owe," I insisted, and pulled out a few crinkled dollar bills from my navy blue Coach crossbody bag.

"Okay, okay," he chuckled and threw his hands up in surrender. "Let me take you out then. That's the only payment I'll accept."

"No, I-" I protested, but he cut me off.

"C'mon, you gotta eat, right?" he said as he grabbed his keys, ready to lock up.

"No, really, I have a lot to get done today, so maybe another time," I told him.

"Chill," he chuckled. "No need to be so uptight,

it's just lunch. Plus, you owe me for this dope haircut my little man is rocking."

I turned to gather our things so we could leave, and Mark took that as his opportunity to talk to my son. Nathan nodded eagerly and Mark appealed to him with thoughts of a Happy Meal and I knew it was game over. Nathan, like most little kids, was completely enamored by Happy Meals so I knew there was no way I could say no without breaking his little heart. Well, at least that's what I told myself.

Mark took Nathan's excitement as a 'yes' and grabbed his coat and keys. It was strange the man was locking up the barbershop in the middle of the day just to take me out, but a small part of me thought it was sweet he was willing to lose income just to spend time with us. We walked down the brick-paved sidewalk to a nearby McDonald's and sat down outside, exchanging personal inquiries of one another over lunch.

"Every kid's weakness is a Happy Meal," Mark chuckled once we settled in a booth at McDonald's.

"Right?" I grinned, watching Nathan fiddle with the miniature Spider Man toy that accompanied his meal.

"I don't get it. So, what makes you happy?"

Mark asked me. He was looking right into my eyes with a piercing stare and the cute smile on his face distracted me. His gaze never wavered from mine, which I oddly found exciting.

He came off as someone who was dominating and always took charge, which I noticed when he upsized my meal even though I declined it and insisting where we should sit.

"My son makes me happy," I answered after a long pause.

"I could make you happy too," he smirked. "

"Is that your line?" I giggled. "I've gotta tell you, it's a little lame."

He raised an eyebrow and leaned back in his seat, still not taking his gaze off of me, "But it's true, I think I've found my wife," he said with conviction.

His words played over and over in my head as I got ready for bed later that night. "Can he make me happy? Me, someone's wife?" I mused. I couldn't stop thinking about him.

The days and weeks that followed our first encounter together were filled with Mark visiting my workplace, taking my son and me out to the movies and extravagant restaurants, sending flowers, buying me random gifts and basically inserting himself in every part of my life. I oddly felt as though he was marking his territory with how persistent and present he was. I'd look to my left or my right, and there he'd be. He was everywhere.

For someone who worked two jobs, he had an awful lot of free time. At one point I felt suffocated. All the boundaries I set seemed to have fallen on deaf ears as he did whatever he thought was best for me without ever consulting me... but for some odd reason I thought it meant he cared.

We got married a few months later. It was a wild romance that kept me on my toes. Our lives seamlessly assimilated to one another's. Plus, I had his baby on the way.

～

Mark moved in with Nathan and me in my apartment before we got married. Although we both had jobs, our income was barely enough to survive on with a kid and another on the way, so we had to do what was necessary to save money until things got better, which was Mark's idea, and it kind of made sense.

Within months, we had explosive fights frequently. I didn't see the sarcastic and argumentative side of him until I became pregnant and we were living together. It seemed as though I was under a microscope. Anything I did or said would be taken out of context and send him into a rage. I brushed off his sudden toxic behavior and always apologized so the fight would end. Even though we argued a lot, the fact we struggled together erased the negative aspects of our relationship.

We were driving home one Sunday after a hearty dinner at my sister Michelle's house when the car suddenly tilted to one side and jerked violently until we came to a complete stop. Mark and I looked at each other with puzzled expressions on our faces. Luckily, Nathan was still sound asleep in the backseat while all this was going on.

Mark got out to inspect the car and came back shaking his head, "It's a flat," he said, and balled his fists up in frustration. We were both dead broke and Mark needed the car to get to work the next day so we were in a bind. I ran my fingers through my long black wavy hair, trying to think of solutions.

"Maybe we dropped some change in the car," I mumbled absentmindedly.

"I pray to God you're right," Mark replied with

renewed hope and searched under his seat. I opened the glove box and did the same.

We could not contain our excitement each time we found a penny. It was a miracle we didn't wake Nathan up. After a thorough search in every nook and cranny, we huddled together under the dim light to count what we found. Our faces lit up when we finished counting, "25 cents!" Mark cheered. It was enough to put air in the tire.

"That's so crazy," Mark chuckled when we were back on the road en route to our home.

I looked at him and smiled, wishing our lives would always be filled with adventures like this one where we were on the same team. It was in these moments I saw the man I fell in love with; the man who pursued me relentlessly. Just the fact we could stick together through thick and thin was all the proof I needed to know we would make our marriage work no matter what... sadly, I was mistaken.

ROSE TINTED GLASSES

"Did you see that plate?" I heard someone whispering on my way to the kitchen.

"My man would never embarrass me like that," another person added.

My sister was hosting Thanksgiving dinner, so it was a grand affair. The table was arrayed with Southern buttermilk fried chicken, candied yams, collard greens, peach cobbler, etc. Holiday music played gently in the background paired with the early Christmas décor created a warm ambiance. The house was booming with laughter and everyone was dressed in their Sunday best. Because it was Thanksgiving, I wondered why everyone was whispering about a person who stacked up their plate with food.

"Aren't you going to say something to him?" Michelle asked me as soon as I entered the kitchen. She was visibly irritated, but I didn't know what she was referring to. "Mark," she clarified, "I'm talking about Mark."

"Did he do something?" I asked her, suddenly feeling concerned.

Michelle rolled her eyes and threw her hands up in frustration, "Sis, it seems like he's trying to finish off all the food by himself. He filled two plates with enough food to feed four people!"

I quickly put two and two together and realized everyone at the dinner were whispering about him. "And what are you wearing?" Michelle continued, "What's going on with you Charlie? Is everything okay?"

"Everything is just perfect," I smiled awkwardly, but I knew it wasn't true.

Mark went from relentlessly pursuing me, showering me with attention and words of affirmation to flat out ignoring my existence at times. He loved to treat himself to expensive name-brand clothing every time his paycheck came through. The man was always decked out from head to toe in Louis Vuitton, Gucci, Prada. You name it, he had it. He was walking around looking all kinds of expensive while I, his pregnant wife, had to make a belt out of a rubber band to keep my pants up because I could not afford maternity clothing. I was six months pregnant with our son so there were things I needed, but my income was minimal, so there wasn't much in excess after my contribution to the household bills and Nathan's monthly daycare expense. However, any extra money Mark had, he'd spend on himself and I could say nothing because he made it abundantly clear it was his money and he could do whatever he pleased with it. People probably thought we were a joke when we were standing next to each other because he looked expensive and well taken care of, but my appearance was on the other end of the spectrum.

For this reason, I felt self-conscious walking up to him because people were already looking in our direction and whispering. My clothes must have given them something more to talk about besides the mountain of food on Mark's plate, and yet he kept piling more on top. I knew candied yams were his favorite, but that didn't mean he had to help himself to the entire dish.

"Honey," I lowered my voice and tried to be as polite as possible, "I think we should probably leave some for the other guests."

I said "we" so it wouldn't sound like I was

blaming him or trying to embarrass him. Mark always picked petty fights with me and I didn't know what would set him off, so I had to talk to him in the sweetest voice possible and with a smile on my face.

"Well, your sister shouldn't host a dinner if she doesn't have enough to feed everybody," he scoffed and walked off with three plates.

My sister, who had been observing our exchange, walked up to me and said, "Charlie, are you really letting him talk to you like that?"

"No, no, he's just a little grumpy because he skipped lunch," I lied. I became accustomed to making up lies for him on the spot so people wouldn't think ill of him or myself for allowing him to treat me so bad. I honestly thought I was protecting our relationship by preserving his public image.

"And your clothes?" Michelle asked, "Is that fine too?"

"It's fine. I'm okay," I lied again to pacify my sister, but she wasn't having it.

"It's unacceptable," she complained, "I can't let my sister walk around looking like this."

Michelle wanted to confront him about it, but I stopped her because I knew how stubborn Mark was and how protective she was. Therefore, it wouldn't end well. It took my mother sitting him down and explaining things to him that made him buy me maternity clothes. I imagine nothing would have changed had she not intervened.

Mark's favorable response to purchasing maternity clothes resulted from embarrassment to his faux persona as the "perfect guy" rather than it being the right thing to do as a man. He was all about maintaining a pristine public image.

What I got out of this particular situation was a deeper respect for my sister. She stood by me even when I didn't want her to. She was like a foundation, strong, immovable, and keeping me together even when I didn't realize it. I loved how close my sister and I became the older we got. The more I matured, the less our twelve year age gap was apparent. Our bond was strengthened with time, like it should have been from childhood, and I was grateful for that.

Mark worked a lot during my pregnancy. At first, I was proud of his hard-working nature because that meant he could take care of a family. I equated being hard-working to being responsible, but I soon learned the two were not mutually inclusive in his case. He started working longer hours when I fell pregnant, even going as far as volunteering to work on his days off. He'd be gone for so long I stopped waiting for him to come home. He worked six days a week and Sundays off, which was the only time we really saw each other, but even then he'd often go out and do his own thing or put in extra hours at work. It felt as though we weren't husband and wife, but roommates.

All the little things he would do when he was courting me completely ceased. We no longer went on dates or other things couples did. He took me out to eat if it was a restaurant he really wanted to try and if he bought me something it was always something that would benefit him too. It was all about him. While all this was happening, my pregnancy was not going as expected. The stress had taken its toll on my mind and body. I kept getting contractions, and because I already had a child, I knew these were not Braxton Hicks because of their intensity.

"Mark," I cried, "Mark, something isn't right."

"Stop being dramatic. You ain't the first person to be pregnant." He rolled his eyes.

"No, no, I'm serious," I pleaded. "It hurts bad."

"Just take the pills the doctor gave you. I'm late for work." He brushed me off.

Mark went to work even though I begged him not to because I was not okay, so I called Michelle and she suggested I go to the hospital immediately. She not only dropped whatever she was doing to be by my side, but stayed with me for as long as I needed her. By the time we got to the hospital, I felt as though my uterus was about to explode. I couldn't stop crying. But I wasn't only crying because of the pain, I was also crying because I was terrified about the possibility of losing my baby.

"Mrs. Roberts, I need you to stay calm," the doctor said. "You're quite far along in labor so it's too late to stop it."

"Everything will be alright sis," Michelle added. "Just calm down and focus on saving the baby."

"Where's Mark?" I asked her.

"Don't worry, he'll be here." She assured me.

The moment our son was born he was whisked away to the NICU and put into an incubator. Mark came by to see our son and me after work. I was too worried about my son's health, so I brushed aside my frustration with my husband, but I was disappointed in him because he wasn't there when I needed him the most.

"Babe, I came as soon as I could. Are you okay?" he said, looking panicked. I stared at him as he stroked my hair lovingly because it didn't seem like he was the same person.

Mark was not the kind of guy who liked the public display of attention, which is why it confused me he was acting like this overly concerned husband. At one point I thought he was bipolar because his personality would completely switch in public.

They released me from the hospital a week after giving birth. We set up an appointment with the doctor to discuss our son's health. They needed to run more tests to determine how long they would keep him in the NICU.

The shrill ringing of the telephone awakened me at 5 a.m. the following morning. Mark refused to answer it, so I rolled out of bed and answered before it went to the answering machine.

"Hello?" I answered sleepily.

"Hi Mrs. Roberts, it's Doctor Taylor."

"Hi doctor, is everything all right?" I asked, suddenly wide awake. Doctors are great people, but they don't call you at 5 a.m. to give you good news. I could hear the loud pounding of my heart in my ears as my throat tightened from the intense anxiety I immediately felt.

The doctor audibly sighed and my heart dropped, "Your son went into septic shock due to an infection from his breathing tube. I'm sorry to say this ma'am, but he won't make it past today."

I don't remember a word she said after that. It's a feeling I cannot describe, but it is one I wouldn't wish on my worst enemy.

Mark got up to get ready for work and found me sitting by the telephone. I found the strength to tell him what the doctor said. He stood quietly with his arms folded, with his only movement being a slight shake of his head every few seconds.

"Listen, I'll go to work first 'cause you know I just started this job, I can't mess it up," he said after what seemed like hours of silence.

I looked up at him and nodded. It made sense he had to at least let his boss know what was going on. I called my sister and Mark's mother to let them know what happened, and they both said they'd come to the hospital. Mark's mother offered to pick me up so I wouldn't be alone.

Each step I took in the hallways of the hospital was torture. I didn't want to get to the NICU because I hoped it was all a terrible dream, but the moment I walked through the doors and saw my son, I felt a part of me die a slow death.

I held his little fragile body in my arms and wept. Michelle and Mark's mother each put a hand on my shoulders to comfort me, but I never felt more alone. All I could see was my son at that moment. I traced my finger along his tiny face, memorizing every little detail about him.

We had been at the hospital for a few hours and Mark still hadn't arrived. His mom called his office and asked for him, but they said he was out making deliveries. She tried again a little while later and got the same response. This made Michelle extremely angry.

"I need to speak to Mark Roberts please," she tapped her foot impatiently. "Listen, I don't care where he is. Y'all better send somebody to get him off the streets 'cause he needs to be here right now."

We couldn't hear the other end of the conversation, but judging by the look on my sister's face, they were not responding how she wanted them to, and I knew she would pop off if they didn't do what she was asking.

"No, you listen to me mister," she continued, "Mark's baby is dying right now and we're at the hospital, so I don't give a damn about no deliveries. Send someone to get him right now."

After a few seconds she said, "Thank you," and I knew that she had gotten her way. I couldn't believe Mark prioritized work over his own child, and this made me very bitter. I was so bitter I didn't even want him to come at all because it felt like we were nagging him, and I didn't want that energy around my son.

Mark showed up and asked to hold our son. He had only been there for exactly five minutes, and then our son died. Our son died in Mark's arms; something none of us ever imagined happening.

~

A couple days later, there I sat in my bedroom thinking about how to get through the day.

Mark walked into the room and unbuttoned his shirt.

"Now, how about we do a little somethin' somethin," he said seductively and started kissing my neck.

I pushed him off me and moved away from

him, "Our son just died a couple days ago and all you can think about is sex?"

"Why are you always trippin?" he replied with a frown on his face, "Women like you are the worst. You don't want to have sex with me, but if I go get it somewhere else, it's a problem."

I sighed and shook my head, knowing there was no getting through to him. "You're unbelievable," I told him before I stormed out of the room.

I could not believe his lack of empathy. Not once did he shed a tear or even look upset. And every chance he got, he blamed me for our son's death, and for that, I loathed him.

Michelle walked in, looking confused and said, "People are blowing up the phone for the location of the funeral."

I frowned in confusion and tried to recall if I told anyone about the death of our baby. It was so traumatizing, I couldn't bring myself to tell people. "What are you talking about?" I asked her.

"Leslie called and said she saw it in the paper," she replied.

I walked to the kitchen with Michelle in tow and pulled out the Washington Post, and sure enough there was a notice about our baby's funeral in the obituary section. My sister and I looked at each other and back at Mark, who just walked into the room fully dressed and announced the limo arrived.

"Limo? What Limo? Mark, what the hell is going on," I asked him.

"My mom planned everything for you," he said nonchalantly, "Let's go."

It turns out Mark's mother, Carol, planned an elaborate funeral for our baby... without my consent. When we arrived at the church she was falling out on the floor and wailing all by herself while everyone watched her with confused expressions. She kept dramatically pretending to faint and asking people to fan her. It was like watching a Broadway show in which she was the star.

Mark's younger brother, Shaun, stood off to the side, leaning against the wall because he couldn't fit in the pews. He weighed about 650 pounds. They all shared a common gluttonous trait that honestly worried me.

Mark's mother got up to do the eulogy and spoke as if my baby lived a long fulfilling life. I always respected her because she was my mother-in-law, but also because she was a minister. It was only after I married Mark I found out she ran a ministry from her basement and called her congregation her "followers."

I should have taken my mother's words seriously when she came back home after first meeting Carol and said, "Something's not right about that woman." My mom told me she tried to "prophecy" to her while holding a cigarette in one hand and a glass of Courvoisier in another.

Carol labeled me as "ungrateful" for all she did for me because she expected me to praise her and show gratitude after the funeral. She stopped talking to me after that day and acted like I didn't exist for years to follow whenever I saw her. It was obvious how similar her behavior was to Mark's.

Nothing was the same after the death of our son. I resented Mark with every fiber of my being for how cruel he treated me during my pregnancy. I couldn't stand being in the same room as him, not to mention the sight of him. However, after consulting with numerous divorce attorneys, I discovered that the state of Maryland doesn't recognize mental cruelty as grounds for divorce. My only recourse was to channel all my anger and bitterness into school and work. Keeping myself busy distracted me and calmed my mind. I was working full-time and attending school six days a week.

I couldn't afford a sitter so I would take little Nathan to school with me on Saturdays and sit him in the hallway outside my classroom with his Gameboy and McDonald's which kept him busy and quiet. I would check on him regularly to make sure he was okay, and each time he'd greet me with a big toothless smile that melted my heart.

My days were so long I barely saw my husband. My schedule ran from 7 am to 10 pm and Mark worked two jobs, and when he wasn't working he wasn't home, but I didn't care. I wanted to leave him anyway.

3

HORSING AROUND

Eight years had now flown by. After the death of our son, God blessed us with a beautiful baby boy who we named after Mark and call Junior. My job put me through college and upon graduating they promoted me multiple times which tripled my income. I also purchased and managed my very own rental property in DC and renovated it. That was something I took so much pride in since Mark forbade me to do it and when I did he refused to help out. Although we were living fairly comfortably, the arguments and verbal abuse became even worse.

Michelle called me one day and said "One of my patients just gifted me a horse and invited me to an event at the stables she boards him at which is a few minutes outside of the city." She went on to add she would like me to join her. I in turn extended the invitation to my childhood friend Raquel. Growing up, she was always intrigued by nature so I was certain she would be delighted to go.

"At last!" Michelle giggled excitedly when we arrived at the stables.

I looked up from my phone and marveled at the sight before me. It brought back so many memories of when I was a kid and would visit my late grandmother's farm in Pennsylvania.

"Mmmm, this feels like grandma's farm," Michelle sighed. "Those were the days when we had not a care in the world," she reflected. I nodded in agreement.

It was indeed breathtaking. But unlike grandma's farm, this place was filled with tons of people and the majority of them were black. I had never seen so many black people on horses before.

The atmosphere was reminiscent of the Deep South. Music was playing in the background as children ran about participating in tag and enjoying the mega-sized moon bounce. Some folks were off to the side playing games of corn hole and horseshoes, while others were attentively grooming their horses and saddling up to head out for a trail ride.

I excused myself to use the restroom, but really I just wanted to get a closer look at the horses. They looked so majestic. As I inquisitively made my way around the stables, I was enamored by the sight of chickens and ducks casually passing my path. I couldn't help but internalize the biggest grin as childhood memories with my grandmother crept in.

"If you're riding, you better hurry up and mount. The group is heading out shortly. We don't want to leave anyone behind," a tall, lean man with olive-toned skin and curly hair that escaped a wide-brimmed western hat, said to me while mounted on the most gorgeous Black quarter horse.

"I'm not riding. I'm just visiting," I said with complete sadness and at the same time, looking up to him in adornment.

"Ok, welcome! My name is Knight. I hope you enjoy your visit."

As he moved on, he made way in my vision a plethora of men, women and children on horseback off in the near distance. It was the most breathtaking sight. Immediately, I returned in the direction of Michelle and Raquel to make sure they got a glimpse.

As I approached ... "Well, there you are Charlie. We've been looking all over for you," said Michelle. "I spoke to the owner about boarding my horse here and he happened to mention he has a horse for sale for a very reasonable price and he'd be perfect for a beginner."

My eyes opened wide with enthusiasm at just the thought of owning a horse. I have always wanted to own a horse of my very own one day. "Who do I speak to? Where is he," I asked her.

"I already figured you'd be interested so I made arrangements for you two to meet tomorrow at 3 pm so you can view the horse and discuss price, etc.," Michelle explained.

As we continued to talk, a stately metallic-orange vintage 1990 Dodge Ram pickup truck with a 4 in lift and over-sized off-road tires, occupied by two women, pulled into a parking space beside us. Raquel pointed at one of the women who exited. She was dressed in full English rider regalia.

"Well, isn't she fancy."

"Yeah, yeah, all that is great, but if I could have that tiny waist, though!" I added.

"Girl, look at her friend. She looks stuck up," Raquel teased.

The two interesting-looking women were polar

opposites, but somehow they had the same vibe. The one dressed as an English rider was petite with the most beautiful caramel skin and the other was seemingly posh with an eye-catching rawhide boho bag.

Raquel and I roamed around the 175-acre farm, checking out the horses and making small talk with people we came in contact with while Michelle was getting her new horse moved-in and learning about the farm rules from other boarders.

As the sun set, we heard amplified sounds of clip-clop, clippity clop approaching us. It sounded like a stampede. In actuality it was people re-turning from the trail-ride that commenced earlier in the day.

Just as Raquel and I were moving out of the way to clear a path for riders returning ,we noticed a young lady walking around with a megaphone announcing they were about to start a bonfire and line dancing.

"You ladies care for some blue juice?" a male voice interrupted us as we were taking it all in.

"Blue Juice?" Raquel and I questioned in unison.

"Yea, Blue Juice! It's my special moonshine. Try it," he chuckled. "I see you ladies are new around here and I want to be hospitable. By the way, if you need anything, my name is Donald." Donald handed us each a small translucent white plastic disposable cup and began to pour a liquid that resembled blue Kool Aid from a metal flask.

Unexpectedly, out of nowhere, music lyrics resounded from surrounding speakers.

Out in the country past the city limits sign

Where there's a honky tonk near the County line

The joint starts jump-in' every night when the sun goes down

They got whiskey, women, music and smoke

It's where all the cowboy folk go to boot scooting boogie

.....Oh heel toe docie doe come on baby lets go boot scootin'

Donald chugged down what remained in his cup, placed the flask in his waistband, and motioned for Raquel and I each to grab an arm and join him on the dance floor.

Without a word said, we accepted his dance invitation by clutching his arms and joining him in on the fun. Within seconds, the dance floor was packed with children and adults positioned in five or more rows of single file lines, moving in synchronicity to a choreographed dance with repeated sequence.

Smoke from the bonfire filled the air and oversized rustic flames luminance of yellow and orange were so bright it lit up the crowd in which I could see Michelle stumbling while making her way towards us.

"You're tipsy!" Raquel teetered while pointing at Michelle.

"I'm definitely driving on the way back," I said, as the only sober person in our trio.

A tap on my shoulder surprised me from a gentleman followed by a friendly introduction. "Hi, I'm Anthony," he said.

"Y'all see this fine man, right? It's not just me?" Raquel whispered a little too loudly as if he couldn't hear while stumbling out of sync on the dance floor. "Is he talking to us," she slurred.

The man completely ignored our antics, joined us and confidently continued his conversation. "You're my kind of people," he exclaimed as best he could over the loud music.

When we asked why he wanted to hang with us he simply shrugged and said, "I like gorgeous women." It turned out Anthony worked at the stables part-time as a horse trainer. He also was extremely popular amongst both men and women as evident by all the random people who kept approaching him.

"I take it you're single then?" Raquel asked

him. "We are flattered but, I'm sure you noticed those beautiful women over there who have been ogling you for the past half hour?" I added.

Anthony looked in the direction I pointed and flashed the women a charming smile and then he turned back to me and said, "Honey, I bat for a different team." We both stared at each other for a brief moment and then burst into a fit of laughter. I never pegged him for a gay guy because he didn't carry himself like the stereotypical characters we saw on TV.

To our left, I recognized the two women looking in our direction as the women we saw earlier exiting the vintage pickup truck. As if he was a mind-reader, Anthony walked over to them and invited them to join us. It was hilarious because the guy who invited himself over was inviting more people. I hadn't fully figured him out, but I liked him already.

"This is the lovely Crystal," he gestured to a light fawn-colored woman with waist-length locs tied with an Aztec and feather print bandana. "And my pretty haute hunter jumper over here is Bianca." Bianca had the smallest waist any woman would die for and a speed bump for a bootie clearly highlighted in her tan English breeches.

And just like that, we went from an intimate

trio to a party of six. Without hesitation, Anthony grabbed my hand and pulled me to the center of the dance floor where we all joined in on the line dancing. I felt my phone vibrate so I retrieved it from my back pocket to view the notification.

Mark: Why the fuck aren't you answering your phone, dude?

Me: I have no missed calls from you. The reception is bad here at the stables. I can't wait to tell you about my day. It was amazing. I'll be home within an hour.

Mark: Tell someone else that bullshit. Ain't nobody at a stables this time of night. Fuck with me bitch and you'll have hell to pay.

Although my mood was tainted by the text exchange with Mark, I refused to let it get me down, so I painted a smile on my face and enjoyed the reminder of my time. It turned out to be one of the best days of my life and I didn't want it to end.

* * *

Michelle: Sis, don't forget the meeting I set up between you and the stable owner at 3 pm. Let me know how it goes.

It was a Sunday so I made sure to complete all my chores and make dinner before my meeting at the stables. I didn't want any reason for Mark to have something to fuss about or give me the silent treatment.

I rounded up the boys and headed to the stables. As I pulled into the parking lot, I noticed the road turned from 'paved' to 'gravel'. The sound of gravel hitting the undercarriage of my car was music to my ears. Boy did this bring back memories of grandma's farm. Once we exited the car, I took a deep breath and inhaled the smell of horse manure which was euphoric to my senses.

"Charlie?" a tall white man with the most electric blue eyes and blonde hair questioned me. There were two Australian Cattle dogs accompanying him.

"Yes, pleased to meet you!" I answered while extending my arm for a handshake.

"I'm Joey, welcome to Piscataway Stables. I hear you're ready to purchase your first horse. I think I have the perfect gelding for you."

Joey and I continued to discuss pricing and boarding options. Once I confirmed I was ready to buy, he ushered me up a steep splintered-wooden staircase atop a two-story red barn. Once we reached the landing, a gentleman with a keen likeness to Joey, opened the door for us to enter as he was leaving out.

"Hi ma'am, my name is Nick. I'm Joey's brother.

You must be Charlie. Pleased to meet you. Welcome to Piscataway Stables. Let me know if I can be of any assistance to you in any way." Joey and I continued into the shed-like office and seated ourselves at a metal desk enhanced with hammered characteristics to finalize the transaction.

Before I knew it, I purchased my first horse. After spending just one night with the horse-riding community, I knew without a doubt this was the medicine I needed in my life. What was even more beautiful is I met three wonderful people who I felt privileged to call my friends. I didn't think my life had any more room to accommodate new people, but my girls didn't need me to make room for them, instead they embraced and made room for me in theirs. When I was with them I could just be Charlie and that was enough. It felt like home to me.

4

COWGIRL CONFESSIONS & PINKY PROMISES

As the years progressed, the five of us became inseparable. No matter how busy, we made it a ritual to meet on the third Sunday of each month for brunch, followed by a trail-ride.

I was the first one to show up at the Cheesecake Factory for our monthly brunch date. Growing up, my father hated tardiness, so it was ingrained in me to always show up early for everything. Plus, I enjoyed watching each friend walk into the room.

The first one to arrive was Crystal. Crystal was our resident fashionista. She was always dressed to the nines with an elegant touch of the most feminine class. Her favorite statement pieces were pearls and leopard print. She had beautiful waist-length locs that emitted the scent of rose water. Crystal always radiated positive energy. However, she was also the most reserved of the group. Crystal was the kind of person who only told you what she wanted you to know, but we always had fun making her come out of her shell a little.

Because she was a vegetarian, we frequently accommodated her needs when selecting a restaurant for our meetups. I loved and admired how passionate she was about animal rights as well as her job as an educator.

"Hey girlie!" she greeted me with her 'Crystal' flair, and immediately launched into conversation, as expected.

She was a strong, confident, and independent woman with a vocabulary that could rival that of top scholars. We would be having a great conversation and out of the blue she would drop a bombastic word on us which would have us Googling the definition on our phones under the table, so we coined her the "wordsmith" of the group.

When we called her out on it, she simply chuckled and said, "What you mean to say is, grandiloquent. Actually, you could add sesquipedalian to that..."

We all burst out in laughter because of how

ridiculous she sounded. I loved her sense of humor and how she was not afraid to make fun of herself. She was an amazing person to be around, especially when you needed a mood-booster.

Next to walk in was Bianca. Although she was petite standing just shy of 5 ft tall, she had a big personality. Bianca was a woman who turned heads, you just couldn't ignore her. She had a strong aura of confidence.

Crystal was funny and bubbly, but Bianca was easily the comedian of our group. Her thick Southern accent and side-splitting humor often fooled people into believing they could walk all over her, but boy were they wrong. Bianca had a take charge, know-it-all attitude, so she was not afraid to put people in their place. This was a helpful trait because her job as an executive at a Fortune 500 company needed her no-nonsense approach.

Bianca was the "Southern Belle." Unfortunately, she couldn't be with us in person all the time because of her demanding job that often required international travel, or she would be spending time with her husband and daughter. She would often attended our get-togethers via FaceTime, and even then she would make us laugh so hard tears would roll down our faces.

Raquel arrived shortly after Bianca. She and I had known one another the longest, since childhood. She, too, commanded attention when she walked into the room. Unlike the rest of us, Raquel had an earthier, eccentric vibe, which only added to her magnetic presence. There was just something about her that made you not only want to pay attention to her but want to know who she was. Her presence was nothing less than elegant. I guess that was one of the reasons she could land wealthy men and have them falling head over heels in love with her.

Raquel was quite captivating with her long hip-length locs and alluring big, bright 'Bambi' eyes, and an inviting lavish body oil scent.

Everything about her complimented her beliefs, from her handmade jewelry with healing crystals to her bohemian styled clothing. But oh, if you could hear her sing. Raquel had a beautiful, sultry, and yet high-pitch sound. It was quite an Erykah Badu-Esque voice that could transport you to another dimension from the first note. She would randomly belt out lyrics to a song that was relative to our topic of discussion.

Most people knew Raquel as a spiritual healer with a home-based beauty business, but she was actually a highly intelligent woman with a master's degree in mathematics and a background as an educator. I loved how sweet and humble she was.

Raquel was the person who kept me the most grounded and centered. She had this calming effect on people and was always sensitive to the energies around her. It wasn't unusual to see her break out a deck of tarot cards every now and then.

Last, but certainly not the least, walked in Anthony, and as usual, the ladies in the restaurant swooned. He was a very handsome man who looked like he was of middle-eastern descent. Women at other tables were adjusting their cleavage and puckering their lips suggestively, but Anthony walked past them without as much as a glance.

"Damn, bitches be too thirsty up in here!" he exclaimed when he got to our table and we burst into fits of giggles when the women checking him out turned away in disappointment.

Our dearest Anthony was openly gay, which you could only tell once he opened his mouth. Not only was Anthony the most dramatic member of our friend group, but he was also sassy, sensual, and had an attitude that went from zero to a hundred real quick. Although he was easily offended,

Anthony loved the easy-going, light-hearted banter we had in our group.

Anthony was the protector. He was always looking out for us. He was a horse trainer by profession, who was widely respected in the equestrian community. The men in the community were kind to him and often joked they became friends with him just so they could get close to pretty women, which Anthony later told us. Apparently, the men jokingly called us Anthony's 'angels'.

If sexy was a person, it would be Anthony. He would often tear up the dance floor with his amazing dance moves that almost always became sexually animated until all eyes were on him. One thing I admired about Anthony was he was not ashamed of his sexuality. While most people felt shy and reserved about their sexuality, Anthony openly flaunted it. A bonus for us ladies was he would often give up sex tips from a guy's viewpoint.

"... So, was it like a nibble or a full-on bite?" Anthony asked Bianca, who just told us a rather graphic story of the new tricks she and her husband been trying in the bedroom, but she stopped at the juiciest part.

"A lady never tells," Bianca coyly sipped her wine.

"A lady in the streets and a freak in the sheets!" Crystal cheered, and we all laughed.

Looking around at my friends tugged at my heartstrings. They had been with me through thick and thin, even though I had not divulged all the information about my marriage, they always knew when I needed a mood-booster and wouldn't push me too hard for explanations even though I could tell how badly they wanted to know.

"Is everything alright?" Raquel asked me, but it sounded like she knew the answer already. I didn't realize Raquel had noticed until she sat next to me.

"Yeah, sis, everything is great," I lied with a fake smile on my face.

"I don't know. Something just feels off about your energy today. You know you can tell me anything, right?" she said sincerely.

"Of course, I do," I nodded.

She smiled sadly and added, "You don't have to be in a situation that steals your light. Remember that."

She was the only one who could see right through me, but she never forced me to do or say anything I wasn't ready for.

I felt like I was supposed to be a ride or die and

stick with him through everything, but also, could I handle the stigma that came with being a divorcee? I didn't even want to think of what everyone would say, especially since everyone was convinced Mark was such a great guy. But most of all, I didn't want to be seen as a failure. Everybody considered us as "couple goals" and praised us for representing black love well, so it felt as though I'd be letting down our community as well.

～

The sun had long set, which meant it was time for us to go our separate ways, but I didn't want to face the reality waiting for me at home so I made every excuse I could think of to prolong my time with the girls.

"Let's continue this at Bianca's house and have Cowgirl Confessions night!" I suggested.

"I'm with Charlie," Raquel chimed in. "I say we take this party to Bianca's house."

"Well, my husband is out of town," Bianca replied with a naughty smile on her face.

"Anthony?" I fluttered my eyes at him.

"Do you even have to ask?" he scoffed.

"Yes! Let's do it," Crystal conceded.

We stopped by the nearest grocery store to

stock up on wine and snacks to take over at Bianca's place. The five of us were sipping on wine while sitting on the plush carpet in Bianca's lounge later that night after watching a chick flick when Crystal suddenly asked the group, "Ok....It's time for Cowgirl Confessions. What's your craziest relationship story?"

Now, I had only been in a couple relationships before Mark, so I could vividly remember the craziest relationship I had been in. "I'll go first," I offered.

"I started dating this guy back in high school. My parents transferred me to a public school from Catholic school, so it was a whole new world for me," I chuckled.

"You discovered that good good," Anthony stuck his tongue out while grinding.

"Anyway," I rolled my eyes at him, "Kevin- that was his name- would do things like give me $500 when I said I was going to grab a pizza with a friend. He bought me a brand new BMW with some dope rims."

"Girl, this sounds like Kevin was doing something illegal?" Bianca said in the most hood accent I'd ever heard and we all burst out laughing. She was always so prim and proper this shocked us all.

"Hush, Y'all need to stop so I can finish this

story," I said between laughs. "So, one day he says he wants to open up to me and takes me to his momma's house. Nobody was home when we got there so he went to turn the light on and it wouldn't come on and pulled out a gun thinking somebody was after him, but it turned out the power was cut off."

"Girl, you are lying," Anthony gasped. "He had a gun?"

"I bet he was in one of those gangs," Crystal shuddered.

"He was a drug lord, actually," I corrected. "Long story short, he got arrested, and it was a big deal in the city and all over the news. I was subpoenaed and testified in front of a grand jury."

"Girl, how on earth are you still normal after going through all that?" Raquel asked me.

"I don't know," I shrugged.

The night went on and everyone told their stories, but they all agreed mine was by far the craziest. Something within me was urging me to open up about how Mark had been treating me for years, but then they complimented me on building a strong and healthy family after that situation, so I kept the truth to myself.

We sipped on wine as we settled into a comfortable silence as each of us reflected on what we had been through individually and as a group. Our friendship was definitely an unlikely one; no one would have ever paired the five of us together. But our differences united us and made us better people. We balanced each other in ways none of us would have expected or hoped for.

"Let's make a promise," Crystal broke the silence, as if she was reading my mind. "Let's swear to always be there for each other no matter what. I know we're a crazy bunch, but the universe brought us together for a reason."

"I agree," Raquel chimed in. "This is a sisterhood like no other. I don't know what I would have done without you all."

"Pinky promise!" I exclaimed in a sing-song voice.

Anthony raised his eyebrows at my outstretched pinky and looked at the rest of us as though he was trying to confirm we were all seeing this. "I love you Charlie, but we're not five. I'd much rather drink to that."

"Alcohol is never the answer," Bianca teased.

I leaned forward and joined my pinky to Crystal's with an encouraging smile on my face. Raquel and Bianca followed suit and we all stared at Anthony who was the remaining piece of the puzzle. He rolled his eyes and sighed dramatically but joined us, nonetheless. Crystal squealed and then composed herself and smiled at the four of us and said, "No matter what happens, or where life takes us, we will always be there for one another. We'll laugh together, cry together, and carry our burdens together. Sisters to the end."

"Sisters to the end!" we said in unison as the four of us locked pinky fingers.

5

IF THE TRAILS COULD TALK

I t seemed like the third Saturday of the month couldn't approach fast enough. Thinking about seeing my girls and going on our monthly trail rides had me thrilled. They had no idea how our outings revitalized me after the turmoil I endured at home with Mark. By now, he was not only emotionally and physically abusive, but there were obvious signs he was having multiple extramarital affairs. No matter how much evidence I presented to him, he stood firm on the fact he came home every night and that's all that should matter.

⌁

"Oh shit, it's 10:51 am," I said surprisingly and grabbed my truck keys.

Customarily, we would meet 11 am at the stables and be ready to hit the trails by noon. The hour we had between gave us the necessary time to groom, tack up our horses and adjust our riding gear.

It would be just the five of us. On this particular day, Bianca expressed she wanted our ride to be classy, so we purchased individual plastic wine coolers, cheese, wheat crackers, fresh fruit, and packed them in our saddlebags, and set off into the woods.

Naturally, we drew attention because it was unusual to see a group of cowgirls (Anthony included) especially so close to the city, so people would stop on the side of the road and ask to take pictures of and with us. What piqued the public's curiosity even more was how different we all looked.

Raquel was dressed in her usual bohemian style maxi dress with a corset, western hat and handmade wooden jewelry incorporated into her look. No one could doubt she was the most spiritual of us.

Bianca was an English rider, so she looked very polished and conservative in her favorite beige breeches, black boots, white polo shirt, and a fitted brim ball cap accented with Gucci sunglasses.

Anthony rode in regular urban clothes. So, a pair of jeans, a graphic t-shirt, retro Jordans, and a baseball cap were his go-to unless he was conducting training or participating in an equine event.

Similar to Anthony, I was more on the urban side, but I liked to incorporate western elements into my outfits, so I had on leggings paired with traditional western fringed chaps, a tank top, my "go to hell" hat, and my favorite Gringo western boots. I called it "Urban chic."

Last, but definitely not the least, was Crystal. She was in a league all on her own with her eclectic flair. She liked Edwardian period-style outfits with a hint of urban and topped off with a silk scarf and broach. For good luck, protection, and homage to her Native American descent, she made sure to add a feather to every hat.

"Over there!" Anthony shouted with excitement. "That's the perfect spot for us. I'll tie the horses while you girls lay out the blankets.

Crystal raised her hands to the sky and sighed dramatically. "I can feel the spirit of my ancestors!" she exclaimed.

Bianca snorted and pulled Crystal down on

the blanket she had laid out. "Girl, sit your ass down. What would your ancestors be doing up on a hill?"

"Having a barbecue?" Anthony snorted.

"That's a racist and stereotypical comment," Crystal rolled her eyes. "But you know what, nothing can bring me down. I feel like my forefathers were chiefs in one of the tribes, you know? I don't get offended easily, and that's queen behavior."

"Well, all right, queen. Do you want some hot sauce with that?" Raquel teased, while ironically holding a bottle of hot sauce.

"Enough with the royalty and hot sauce," I chimed in. "I want to know what y'all have been up to lately."

As we all simmered down and lay on our backs marveling at the splendor of the beautiful night sky arrayed with billions of stars, we stayed in the catching up on life for a few hours until Raquel called us to attention and said "It's getting late. We should start heading back. Let's hold hands and have a moment of silent prayer."

Once finished, we we mounted our horses and Anthony said "I'll lead the way back. Plus, I need to control the pace so you bitches can hear this tea I was saving for last."

Crystal's eyes shifted in curiosity and said, "Oh my! I'm all ears."

"I'm scared to ask," said Bianca.

Raquel followed up with "Ha, tell it all. I'm here for it boo."

"Well, ya'll know Lisa's boyfriend has been getting riding lessons from me for the past six weeks." Well, those aren't the only lessons he's been getting.

We all gasped in amazement.

"I would have never, in a million years, pegged him to be bi-sexual. Do you think Lisa has any idea?" I asked.

"Didn't I tell y'all bitches I had some tea? Somebody's man trying to hook up with me ain't tea. The tea is that Lisa was in on it!!!" Anthony exclaimed as he looked back at us to capture our reactions.

Anthony always had a story that kept us entertained.

"I have a question. Before you came out of the closet, you slept with a few women. So...What is good pussy? I want to know what men consider good pussy. "Hell, I think we all want to know what men consider good pussy." Raquel said in curiosity.

"Now that's the million-dollar question we all

want to know," Crystal belted out loudly from the rear of the line.

At this point we collected our horses down to a very slow walk to quiet down the sounds of the brush and leaves under their hooves so we could clearly hear Anthony's response.

"So? Uhmmmm, inquiring minds want to know and we ain't got all night. These mosquitos are tearing my ass up," Bianca uttered sarcastically.

After a deep sigh of teasing, Anthony said "Ok ok ok, I'll tell y'all just this once so listen the hell up. Good pussy is clean, tight, juicy, and has muscle control. If you don't know, muscle control is when you squeeze and release his dick with each and every stroke. And if your cat don't squeeze like it use to, don't worry, you can pop her right back into shape in no time with a set of Yoni eggs. They comes in three sizes so when you get down to size small, that's when you can snatch his whole soul out."

Crystal yelled out to us from the back with an infectious laugh and said "Ladies, I took notes and already ordered my Yoni eggs on Amazon."

Just as we were keeling over in our saddles with laughter, Anthony unexpectedly screams

"The last one back to the barn is a rotten egg," and took off in high gear.

We all immediately followed in pursuit. Hoping to gain first position, I veered off the main path to shorten my distance. The feeling of the wind against my face and the smell of nature as I raced through the woods on my horse was euphoric. To be honest, the wind was not the only thing beating against my face. I was getting slapped left and right by tree branches!

None of that stopped me, though, I was fierce, I was bad, I was sexy like a scene from a movie... until... a branch snatched my wig off.

I had to double back and maneuver my horse to get to it. It was like a whole episode of CSI as I strategized ways to get to the tree to get my wig like my life depended on it. My horse danced around nervously because it looked like I was getting an animal out of the tree.

After a few attempts, I finally grabbed hold of my wig and celebrated my victory. I secured it back on my head and off I went to catch up.

The five of us arrived at the barn seconds apart, one by one. Just as I dismounted my horse, they all looked at me and Anthony said, "Don't think we didn't just see your ass getting your wig out of the tree."

I froze in shock. My girls had no idea, until that moment, I had been wearing a wig. The luscious long thick crown I was known for having was gone. What presented underneath was a thin mane of hair with patches of bald spots. No one knew I resorted to pulling my hair out as a result of stress I was under.

"Did I ever tell you guys about the time my wig fell off during a board meeting?" Bianca said dramatically as she was tying her horse Jack to the hitching post.

Anthony's jaw dropped. "Shut up! No it didn't."

"Girl, It was tragic!" She exclaimed. "I stood up to help the executive assistant with the computer. The poor little thing was messing up a simple Powerpoint presentation."

"And you two had a catfight?" Anthony asked with excitement.

Bianca gave him a sarcastic look and continued with her story. "ANYWAY, I got up to help her because no one else seemed to care and my wig, which wasn't properly secured, got caught in my chair's headrest...and stayed there."

Crystal kept a straight face and pressed her lips together to stifle the laugh that threatened to escape, but then tears rolled from her eyes. Raquel was the first to open the floodgates and the rest of us followed in roars of laughter.

Afterward, we continued on to tell embarrassing hair stories while putting the horses in their stalls for the night. As I listened and laughed, my heart swelled with gratitude towards my girls for not asking about my hair. I knew they were curious but their love and respect for me won over their curiosity and that made me feel like my secret was safe.

I quietly entered the house upon returning home. As I approached the bedroom door, I could hear Mark on the phone telling his friends I was a terrible wife and he was unhappy and wanted to leave me.

"You've been saying that for years, Mark. Why don't you just divorce her and move on?" a female voice said.

The call was on loudspeaker and there seemed to be two other people involved. I couldn't recognize the other man's voice but that was irrelevant. Just listening to the awful things he was saying about me shed light on so many uncomfortable situations I had encountered with his friends and family.

"See this right here?" Mark said while leaning into his phone's camera, "She hit me when I tried to have a conversation about her cheating. She be going out dressed all sexy to get attention from men, and all I was saying was that it's inappropriate to behave that way in front of our children, you know what I mean?"

"You deserve better," the woman replied, "I always knew there was something off about her. I don't know how you can stay with a cheater."

"I do it for the kids," Mark sighed, "I want them to grow up with a dad."

"That's a real man right there," the male voice responded, "But man to man, get you some on the side too. Don't let her play you like that."

I shook my head and willed myself not to cry. Hearing my husband drag my name through the mud and tell vile lies about me for no apparent reason was painful. He had painted himself to be not only a 'good man' but a 'victim'.

6

WHEN LIFE HAPPENS

"Mom, I'm home!" I called out into the seemingly empty house when I arrived.

I was now caring for two terminally ill parents, my eldest son was being scouted as a top division I college football recruit, my youngest son was struggling academically, and I still had other duties to fulfill as a wife. To top it all off, Mark's daughter from a previous relationship was killed in a car accident.

The doctors had given my mother six months to live, so I arranged for her to leave Florida where she and my dad retired, to live with us so she would receive better medical care.

Our puppy- Xena- came bounding down the

stairs to greet me. Xena was a gift to the boys from my mother. She wanted to leave them with something to remember her by and remove the sting of her inevitable death.

I walked into the guest room and found my mother sitting in bed with a book in hand. She looked up at me and smilingly beckoned me to come closer. "Oh, my baby," she brushed my hair gently when I laid my head on her lap.

"I'm a grown woman, Mom," I chuckled even though her words brought me more comfort than I was ready to admit.

"You will always be my baby," she said in her honeysuckle voice. She had a warm, calming tone. Every time she spoke I could hear the courage, strength, and endurance in her voice. Her words always had a story behind them.

"Are you feeling okay?" I asked after a few minutes of silence.

"You know I'm as strong as an ox," she chuckled, "Ain't nothing gone' bring me down. A cup of tea would do me some good, though."

"Hmm, I think I still have some of those butter biscuits you love so much," I mused loud enough for her to hear.

"One or two wouldn't hurt," she replied nonchalantly, which made me giggle. I knew how much she loved those biscuits, even though she was trying to play it cool. Now that I was a mother, I understood her as a person and the sacrifices she made for my sister and me when we were younger.

It's easy to look down on a woman and think she is foolish for staying with a man who is no good for her, but once I got married, I understood why my mother reacted or responded to situations the way she did, not that it was the healthy way, but I understood her reasoning.

I walked back into my mother's room with a plate of two butter biscuits and a glass of milk on her favorite tray. I had this beautiful bronze-colored vintage tray she loved so much.

My mom smiled and lightly patted the spot next to her, so I took my shoes off carefully and got in the bed with her. I felt my body relax as soon as I was next to my mother. This was the relationship I wish we had when I was younger. We would chat about random things for hours and watch her favorite TV shows together when I got home from work.

"I wish I had paid more attention to the signs," my mother sighed and coughed after finishing her glass of milk.

"It's not your fault, Mom," I told her sincerely.

The doctor told us if they caught her illness in its early stages, it would have been curable.

"No, it is," she smiled sadly. "Pay attention to your body, Charlie. Don't wait until it's too late."

"I'm good Mom," I lied. I had been battling issues with my periods for years after multiple miscarriages. It had begun to get worse, but with all that was going on, I had no time to undergo extensive medical testing. Everybody needed me.

My mom shook her head and closed her eyes, which meant she was exhausted. "I see how hard you work, baby," she said. "I know you're doing this alone, but you don't have to."

I kissed her on the cheek and got up to leave the room, "Get some rest," I whispered, thinking she had already fallen asleep.

"Charlie....Find a man who loves you the way you love him," she said in her drowsy state before drifting off to sleep.

"Mark loves me," I replied, even though I knew she was asleep. "He's not perfect, but I know he loves me... I swear."

I was fighting so hard to keep our family together and uphold an image it hadn't dawned on me until that moment I was sacrificing myself in the process. Nathan's academics were thriving and his football career was about to take off, but Junior, on the other hand, was really struggling with his academics, so I was doing all I could to help him.

A lot of things were demanding my time and attention and pulling me in every direction. I was so busy I became emotionally numb. I had no time to cry nor anyone to talk to about what I was feeling. My family needed me to be strong for them, so that's what I did.

~

As the months went by, my mother's health rapidly declined. In those months I had with her, she opened up to me about her regrets and mistakes and implored me not to follow in her footsteps. She encouraged me to love myself enough to choose myself, even though I didn't know how to do that, but she saw in me what I did not see in myself and never ceased to uplift me and reassure me I was doing a good job.

Exactly 6 months from the day my mother received her diagnosis, she was admitted to the ICU. I called Mark and told him to meet me at the hospital. I wasn't expecting him to show up judging by past experiences, but he shocked us all when he walked in.

"Oh my God, it must be really bad for me.

Mark is here," my mom whispered before having a coughing fit.

It was no secret to the family Mark was self-centered. He never really went out of his way for anyone in the family; he only did for strangers so he could keep up his image. So, we were all genuinely surprised to see him there, to a point where it was uncomfortable.

My mom passed away a few days later in the hospital. We knew it was coming, but it didn't make it hurt any less.

"How are we going to tell dad?" I asked Michelle. We were sitting in my living room, finalizing the details of the funeral. Our father was in remission from cancer and had a pacemaker as a result of a prior heart attack, so we didn't know how to break the news about Mom's death to him. We both agreed we couldn't tell him over the phone, so we flew him to DC so we could be there to provide emotional support to him.

When he arrived, he was eager to see her. He kept asking when we were going to the hospital, so we couldn't put it off any longer. Michelle and I led our dad out into the backyard to tell him the news because there were too many people in the house.

"Dad," Michelle began slowly while I held his hand, "Mom died a couple of days ago."

"What," he gasped. "Come on, you're lying to me."

"It's true, Dad," I whispered.

My father looked at me and then my sister as if he was waiting for one of us to drop the act, but when he saw our tear-streaked faces he clutched his chest and began to hyper-ventilate.

"Dad, Dad!" I cried out as he dropped to his knees in agony. A trip he thought was planned to spend time with family was actually to attend his wife's funeral.

The next three months were completely clouded. I was functioning on autopilot. Our father was diagnosed ten years prior with cancer but in remission. However, it returned after our mother's death. Hence, he moved in with Mark and I. There I was repeating the cycle of caregiver for a terminally ill parent while managing two children, a demanding job and husband. He refused all options of treatment and only asked to spend his last days with his grandchildren.

"Dad, I'm home.....Dad!" I called out as I came home from work and placed my keys on the table along with take-out I picked up from Toni's, a local Italian restaurant. They had the most amazing spaghetti carbonara which was my dad's favorite.

Raquel volunteered to pick up the boys after school and take them to the movies so the house was exceptionally quiet.

"Dad!" I called again.

I looked around and noticed Xena our dog didn't greet me when I walked in the house as usual. Immediately a feeling of doom overcame me and grew more intense the closer I approached the split staircase. I took a deep breath with every step I made to ascend the stairs. Once I reached the top I could see Xena sitting outside my father's bedroom door. At that very moment I asked the Lord in silent prayer to give me strength to accept what I knew in my heart I was about to encounter.

"Dad!" I mumbled nervously as I cracked the bedroom door open slowly. And there he laid peacefully. As I looked on at his lifeless body, overwhelmed with grief, I leaned against the wall for added support because my knees felt weak and my breathing became constricted. As I stared, I reflected on memories of him teaching me how to ride a bike and change a tire. He was bigger than life to me growing up. He was far from perfect but still my superhero.

I pulled out my phone and wiped my tears as I dialed Michelle's number.

"He's gone," I sniffled.

"What time did he pass?" Michelle asked.

"I don't know for certain but the time now is 6:12 p.m."

L ife didn't slow down after my dad died. I was so consumed with taking care of my family I didn't realize I hadn't seen my girls in a few weeks. Every time one of them called or texted I would say, "I'll call you back," and only remember to call back hours or even days later.

"Mark!" I called out from the bathroom.

I was instantly crippled by the most excruciating pain in my abdomen so intense I collapsed on the bathroom floor, unable to walk. Mark rushed me to the ER. Shortly after arriving I was taken into emergency surgery.

It turns out I was hemorrhaging internally and had suffered another miscarriage. The doctor called it a "Ruptured Ectopic Pregnancy" and told us it was life-threatening.

Mark was nowhere to be found when I came out of surgery. Not only was I in pain, but I was emotional about everything that happened. I tried calling his phone, but it kept going to voicemail, so I called my sister instead and she came running.

"Where were you?" I asked Mark when he walked into my hospital room later that day.

"I was tired, so I went home to get some sleep," he shrugged. "What did the doctor say?"

I was speechless.

My sister was fuming, but I squeezed her hand and shook my head because I knew they would argue and I didn't have the strength for it. "You look tired, Mark," Michelle said bitterly. "Why don't you go home and get some more rest? I'll take care of Charlie."

It was all too much for me to take, I couldn't get out of bed a few days later. I was emotionally and physically exhausted. Michelle had done an excellent job taking care of me, but she had to go back to her family, and that's when I broke down.

I was sobbing in my bed when the door slowly creaked open. There was no strength left in me to pretend so I couldn't even raise my head to see who had walked in, but when I felt a dip in my bed and smelled a mixture of familiar scents, I knew who had shown up, and then I truly bawled.

"We've got you, sis," Raquel said as she wrapped her arms around me.

"We'll get through this together," Bianca said, and wrapped her arms around me.

Anthony and Crystal came in for the hug as well and then I came undone. I don't know how long I cried, but my friends never once let me go. They sat there and held me while I cried. Their presence pieced me back together.

7

PSYCHO-THERAPY

T he death of my parents had shaken me to the core, but also given me a newfound strength to live my best life. It was as though their death was the wake-up call I needed to get my life and relationships in order. I was not meant to merely survive life but to enjoy living it, and as difficult as my situation was, I was determined to make the necessary changes for my sons and myself.

"What are you doing?" Mark's voice startled me. I nervously shut my journal and put it under a pile of paperwork.

"Just working," I smiled, "How was your day?"

"There's nothing to eat," he said, but it sounded more like a command than a statement.

"I'll get started on dinner soon," I replied. "I didn't expect you home so early."

"So now I have to announce when I'm coming home? A good wife doesn't have to be told when and how to take care of her husband." He chuckled. I didn't find it funny.

I asked him straightforward, "Are you insinuating I'm a bad wife?"

"Lighten up," he chuckled again. "You're so uptight."

I started journaling, and I found it to be immensely helpful, but it wasn't enough, so I did some research and found a highly recommended therapist, Dr. Raine, and booked a session with her. I was skeptical about it, but I needed help and I had to begin somewhere.

Dr. Raine's office felt like a safe space. As soon as I walked in I felt the warmth of the sun streaming in through the large north-facing windows, with its light bouncing off the furniture to create hues of orange and yellow that gave the room an autumn-like glow. Her assistant didn't notice me walk in at first as she was furiously typing something on her computer, which was comical given she worked in a place that was supposed to be calming.

The assistant looked up at me with a puzzled

expression at first, and when it finally registered, I was standing in front of her, she hastily got up and extended her hand in greeting. "Dr. Raine will be with you shortly," she told me before I could get a word in.

"I'm so sorry," she continued, "I know I'm rambling. It's just that it's my first day and I don't really know where anything is because the previous lady just up and left so the doctor had to find a replacement quickly... "

"I'll take it from here, Naomi," Dr. Raine interrupted her and ushered me inside.

I was so amused by her behavior because I remembered how frazzled I was on my first day at work.

"My apologies for that," Dr. Raine said as soon as we stepped into her office, "It's her first day."

"It's alright. I totally get it. We've all been there," I smiled politely.

She pointed to a large emerald green sofa and said, "Please, have a seat. Make yourself comfortable."

"How are you Mrs. Roberts?" She asked.

"I don't know," I told her honestly. "I feel so many things but at the same time I feel nothing."

Dr. Raine put her notebook down and leaned back into her seat. "I get that. Often times we feel overwhelmed to the point of numbness. Can you tell me what it is that makes you feel overwhelmed?"

My voice cracked as I continued. "I'm not okay. I....I don't think I've been ok in years."

"Because ......?" Dr. Raine asked.

"My husband." I nodded tearfully. "My husband is a monster. It's like he's trying to make me lose my mind. He verbally abuses me when he doesn't get his way and blatantly lies about the most trivial things we both know are true. He has made up ridiculous and embarrassing rumors about me to friends and family. Everything I ever told him in confidence has been repeated in casual conversations with others. I can't remember anything and I now suffer from panic attacks."

Dr. Raine nodded as though she was taking mental notes. I noticed she wasn't looking at me anymore but at my hand. I looked down at my hand on the armrest and saw it trembling. I slid my hand under my thigh.

"Sorry." I said awkwardly.

"You don't have to apologize. Hand tremors can be caused by anything from medication to emotional trauma. It's not your fault."

"He laughs in my face whenever I cry and says I'm an Oscar-worthy actress."

"Charlie, I hope you know that's not normal. Your spouse is suppose to love, respect, and support you. He is mentally abusing you."

Tears rolled down my face as I continued to open up and tell Dr. Raine about the affairs, financial abuse and more.

My session went better than I expected. I was relieved to express myself without fear of judgment. It was liberating to know I didn't have to lie or omit some information. By the end of the session, I was already feeling lighter.

There was one statement she made that left me thinking long after I left her office. She said, "People who fail after divorce, didn't plan properly."

I felt like a weight had been lifted off of my shoulders as I drove home. For the first time since I got married, I was completely vulnerable and honest about my relationship with Mark and how it affected me. Dr. Raine would stop me whenever I tried to make excuses for his behavior like I always did and instead asked me to just tell her what happened, exactly how it happened.

~

"**W**here the fuck are you?" Mark barked as soon as I answered my cell phone.

"I'm on my way home. What's the matter?" I asked him, feeling concerned something bad happened.

"Oh, I see," he chuckled, "So you left me here to get everything ready because your pussy was itching for some new dick, huh?"

We often hosted large parties at our home whenever major sporting events were happening. In this case, there was a big boxing match on so we invited our friends, family, and colleagues over to our home for the event.

I immediately pulled the car over and stared ahead in shock. "Mark, what are you talking about? How could you say that to me?" I choked up.

"Listen, you better not walk in this house smelling like some nigga's cum or else." He threatened me.

"Or else what, Mark? What will you do?" I pushed back.

"Try me bitch," he yelled and hung up abruptly.

I took a few deep breaths to calm my racing heart and repeated the mantras Dr. Raine had taught me. "This too shall pass," I began, "My body fills with light and I am calm and stress-free. I am strong. I am powerful. I am beautiful. I am lovable. All is well."

I repeated my mantras until my breathing slowed down and my head felt clearer. Honestly, I was still afraid of what would happen when I got home, but I was no longer filled with anxiety about it.

~

I found several people lounging around drinking beers when I got home and immediately welcomed them over-enthusiastically because their presence meant Mark would be on his best behavior.

More people arrived, and soon a large crowd had gathered. I was running around making sure everything was in order but having to push my way through the throngs of people really slowed me down.

On my way to refill the food trays, I bumped into one of Mark's friends- James. I thought little of it at the time because there were so many people brushing against each other, but later that night as I was cleaning up it suddenly dawned on me, James looked at me in a rather vulgar, disgusted way when we bumped into each other.

For reasons unknown to me, Mark's friends were always cold towards me or they would make little snide remarks that didn't make sense to me. I never really took it to heart because Mark always said, "Chill the fuck out, man. You're always overreacting and acting crazy."

Mark walked into the kitchen as I was packing away the dishes and almost immediately, my heart palpitated. His slow clap and menacing laugh were all I needed to know that I would not be getting any sleep.

"Stupid ass bitch," he began. "So you couldn't even keep your pussy closed for one night, huh?"

"What did I do now?" I asked him, already feeling defeated. Judging by how riled up he was, I knew he was going to go all night yelling and possibly even throwing things. He'd always throw these childish tantrums.

"What did you do now?" he yelled. "Oh, so you're ignorant now? I bet you'll spread your legs for any dick, but they don't know you ain't even got a pussy!"

That was another thing Mark tormented me with. Because of my ruptured ectopic pregnancy, I needed a hysterectomy. It was the only solution to save my life. Mark being Mark, used this as a new way of insulting me every chance he got.

"All is well. This is only for a moment," I whispered to myself repeatedly until Mark was done raining insults on me and walked away.

∼

The evening of the next day, Raquel and I were scheduled to go on an outing. She picked me up because I was in no condition to drive. The anxiety was so overwhelming I found myself unable to function. As if she knew what I was going through, Raquel wasn't her usual chatty self during our drive. She lightly hummed a song I wasn't familiar with as she drove us to our destination.

I can't say I remembered the trip, but the moment we arrived and I looked up at the sky, it was as though a switch was flipped on within me. I listened to calming tones of the insects singing in harmony with the gentle whistle of the evening breeze. I laid on my back with the amethysts Raquel had given me in my hand while focusing on my breathing and clearing my mind.

I don't deserve this.

These words filtered through my ears as clear

as day. My voice, strength, and will to live had been stolen from me.

"I can't fix it," I said out loud. Raquel turned to face me, but she didn't ask any questions.

"I can't fix him," I mumbled to myself.

I went to bed that night thinking back to when Mark revealed who he really was and couldn't believe I missed all the signs. Because we started from nothing, I believed I had to prove myself as a "ride or die" by staying with him even when I began to earn more than him in spite of how he treated me.

We had been going around in circles for so many years, I finally felt exhausted. Maintaining a marriage took work, absolutely, but 'work' was not what it took to maintain Mark and my marriage. It was mentally and physically taxing. I didn't believe that was how marriage was supposed to be. I no longer recognized the woman who stared back at me in the mirror because her eyes looked tired and defeated and that was not who I was or would allow myself to be.

8

TAROT ... TELLS ALL

I called Raquel a few days later and asked her to come over so we could have a Tarot reading session. She had been reading Tarot since college, but I was always afraid to try it. I was in a dark place, needing a bit of direction so I was willing to try anything at this point.

Raquel walked in looking chic, as usual, wearing an African print maxi dress and her locs elegantly styled with a beautiful printed scarf trimmed with sea-shells. Already, I could feel the warmth and positive energy from her aura radiating in the room, and it instantly put a smile on my face.

Per usual, we had girl chat as we sipped on wine. Raquel reached over and pulled out this mini black velvet satchel embroidered with gold stitching of the solar system and says, "Are you ready?" in a mystical voice. I took a deep breath and asked if she could start slow and reveal only one card to start the reading. She flipped a card and said "You would become famous." We turned it into a joke and cackled when Mark walked in.

"I see you ladies are having a good time," he said as he took a couple of sodas out of the fridge.

"Do you want us to take this to another room?" I asked him when I saw him taking more things out of the refrigerator to make a sandwich.

He walked up to me with a big smile and gave me a peck on the cheek, "Nah, you ladies have fun. Don't mind me."

I went back to my seat and Raquel reshuffled the deck of Tarot cards. When finished, she instructed me to touch them and ask a question.

"What is in my near future?" I asked inquisitively.

The suspense I felt was so intense as she flipped multiple cards one by one in an intricate pattern on the table. A part of me wanted to back out in case there was some validity to her interpretations. But I was desperate for answers by any means necessary.

I hinged on the edge of my seat as Raquel

flipped the cards over one by one. I couldn't help but notice she took a while starring at the cards that were revealed and had a perplexed look on her face. "Raquel, what's wrong? What does it mean?" I asked her nervously.

"Wow, Ten of swords!" she said while scratching her head with a bewildered look on her face. "So, the first card of the reading represents the overal energy governing your day to day life. The ten of swords means pain and suffering." She explained.

"Huh? That can't be right," I told her, even though I knew exactly what the card was referring to.

Her eyes slowly moved on to the next one and she seemed even more confused. "The King of Swords in reverse. This signifies a person in your life that is irrational, controlling, violent and cold," she mumbled under her breath awkwardly when she realized Mark was paying attention to what she was saying.

"Now, you have the Seven of Swords. This card indicates there is a person around you who is a thief, cheater, liar and a manipulator," she said as she looked at me worriedly.

Honestly, a part of me wanted her to put two and two together and realize I was living a completely different life from what they all knew. I wanted her to say it out loud for Mark to hear in hopes it would be the catalyst he needed to finally change.

Raquel took a deep breath and looked up at me after glancing at the next two cards.

"You also have The Six of Swords and The Fool. These suggest travel and new beginnings. Basically, a major life change is in your future; like a fresh start in a new city."

She nervously glanced over my shoulder and told me Mark was paying attention to her words. I could see the hesitation written all over her face so I encouraged her to keep going. I don't know where this sudden boldness came from. Usually, I'd stand up to Mark when we were alone behind closed doors, but the Tarot reading was making me feel empowered in that moment.

Raquel shuffled the cards once more and asked me to pick one. I tapped on a card without much thought and she flipped it over and gasped. "The ten of cups," she sighed in relief. "Okay, Sista! Whatever is going on, trust and know when it is all over, you will have abundance and everything your heart desires ."

Raquel scooted forward and whispered, "We should probably stop. It's getting late."

I rolled my eyes and tapped my finger on the table for her to finish the reading. The reading was more intriguing than I imagined. All my fears melted away by the mere hope I would one day get to my Ten of Cups, which was wish fulfillment.

"Okay, okay, one more card," she said after taking a sip of wine. I picked one and this time she paused and frowned. Her silence was so unnerving I fidgeted in my seat.

"Well, what does it mean?" I implored her.

"This card means a new love. It usually signifies a new relationship..." she trailed off. Mark slammed his plate on the counter, startling us. His eyes were focused on the sandwich he was making, but judging by his expression, he was pissed off.

"You know what, I've had too much to drink, so my energy must be fucked up," she laughed nervously and gulped down the rest of her wine before hurriedly collecting her things. "This is the end of the reading. I'm going straight to bed when I get home. Woo, this wine had me talking crazy. Bye, Y'all."

Raquel gave me a quick hug and hurried out the door as though she were in a race. I wanted to walk her to her car, but she was out the door before I even realized what was happening. I looked at my husband, who was still busy with his sandwich, for confirmation that what had just happened was strange, but he was minding his own business.

I got a call from Raquel the next day apologizing for the way she left, and then she told me Mark had called her to elaborate on the Tarot reading, which was beyond strange. I didn't realize he was paying close attention to her words, plus it was something he didn't believe in, so the whole thing was weird.

"I didn't tell him anything more, so don't worry," Raquel assured me.

"Thanks, girl. I guess I'm just shocked he was paying attention in the first place," I replied.

"Are you really okay though?" she asked. All traces of humor had left her voice. It was obvious the cards had revealed to her more than she had let on, but I was not ready to let anyone in Pandora's box. So, I assured her I was fine and ended the call.

9

THE AWAKENING

I didn't know where we were going because all I could see were the streetlights as my mother sped through the streets of Washington, DC. My heart was racing fast and tears welled in my eyes because I could tell she was not okay.

We arrived at a building I was unfamiliar with. My mother scooped me up into her arms and raced to an apartment and locked us in. She kept reassuring me everything was all right, but I could tell she was scared, which terrified me all the more.

We let out panicked screams when we heard a loud banging on the door. My mom held me in her arms and told me the banging would stop if we were silent, but it never did. The longer we stayed still ,the more incessant the banging became.

My mom took my small face in her hands and said, "Listen to me baby, you're a good girl, right?"

I responded with a nod, even though everything in me didn't wanted me to shake my head. "Good," my mother continued, "Now, I want you to hide in the closet, okay? Don't come out until I come for you, baby. You hear me? I want you to be a good girl and be very quiet in there, okay?"

I nodded, but in my head, I was telling her not to open the door. I begged her repeatedly to not open the door, but sadly, my mouth betrayed me by remaining shut. But I continued to beg her in my mind as she put me in the closet and left it open by a crack so I could breathe because I knew there would be trouble when she opened that door.

I watched as my mother took a few deep breaths and then slowly unlocked the door one bolt at a time with trembling hands. When she got the last bolt right at the top of the door, my dad burst through with so much force it sent her flying into a nearby table.

She gathered herself and attempted to run to the bathroom, but his long, quick strides easily caught up with hers and he grabbed her arm and yanked her backward. My mother fell onto the bed with such force I heard a loud crack. My father beat her and ignored her cries for mercy.

My father then went into the bathroom and came

back with a douching bottle. "You really wanna whore around huh?" he slurred drunkenly, "Is this how it felt?!" he yelled and then rammed the bottle in her vagina repeatedly.

I quickly covered my mouth with my hand to stifle the scream that nearly escaped my mouth. I watched from the closet, frozen with fear, as he violently abused her. That was the first time I peed my pants. The shock and horror of it all caused me to lose control of my bladder, yet still, I stayed put just as I had promised.

Relief washed over me when I thought he was done, but his anger was rekindled when she got loose and tried to run out of the room. Again, he caught her, all the while yelling expletives and accusing her of cheating on him.

He took a glass and threw it on the floor, sending shards of glass everywhere. "Walk across the floor," he commanded her, but my mother vehemently refused and tried to get free. He then reached on the dresser and grabbed the Jean Nate aerosol body perfume spray and lit it with his lighter, creating a torch. "If you don't walk across the floor, I'm gonna burn your fucking face off," he snarled.

With tears in her eyes and her body battered black and blue, my mother walked barefoot across the floor littered with broken pieces of glass, and all I could think as I watched that horrific sight with tears *streaming down my face was, "I told you not to open the door."*

~

I woke up in a pool of sweat, screaming and crying after that horrible nightmare. It had taken years for me to get that day out of my mind, but something seemed to have triggered that memory. Oddly enough, it felt like it was a foreshadowing of something to come, and that thought alone gave me chills.

Never had I dwelled on my childhood trauma or put the blame on my parents for the way I reacted to the situation. I learned to lock away all my terrible memories and just focus on living each day as it came. Adding to that, as my parents grew older, they became remorseful for their former actions and worked hard to become better people for each other and their family, so I could not hold their former actions against them.

I replayed my nightmare repeatedly in my mind and saw the parallels with my adult life. Witnessing such a horrific sight at a young age made me almost numb to abuse. It was as though the words my mother said that day, "Be very quiet and stay in the closet," coupled with all the time I spent alone growing up, had caused me to become a person who internalizes everything.

When I looked back on all my years with my husband, I realized even when I got fed up and stood up for myself, I never truly expressed everything I was feeling. It's like I knew no one could understand or deal with it once I opened Pandora's Box because I hadn't really dealt with it either. It had been easier to lock all the painful memories away.

~

A few days later, Mark took me out for a birthday lunch, which would have been dinner had it not been for his busy work schedule. He called me and asked me to meet him Mastro's steakhouse during his lunch break. This would have been a sweet gesture had I not found out he didn't have to work that day but asked his boss for an extra shift.

"Something has been weighing on my mind for some time now," I began carefully. "And I feel like I can't keep waiting for the right time to talk to you. You know I love you and our family, but I'm tired, Mark. I'm tired of fighting all the time. I feel like you don't respect me because of how you treat me and the words you say to me sometimes. This has to change Mark. This has to change, or I'm going to have to file for divorce. We can't go on living like this."

"Is that a threat?" he asked calmly while chewing on a piece of steak.

I closed my eyes and pinched the bridge of my nose in frustration. For once I thought I had actually gotten to him, but I remembered he always put on a "nice" persona when we were out in public.

"I'm not threatening you," I said after a few deep breaths. "I'm asking you to treat me better because I can't live like this anymore."

"Wow," he smiled at me lovingly when the server approached, but when he walked away Mark added, "So now you've got the balls to make threats just because you make more money."

"Are you even listening to me?" I asked calmly, but my patience was wearing thin. "Mark, I'm saying we need to find a way to fix our marriage because this isn't healthy for either of us. If this marriage is hurting us, then it might be for the best we go our separate ways."

"You think you're better than me," he chuckled and sipped his wine. "I always knew you were evil, Charlie, but this is a new low even for you. You're trying to take everything from me. I mean, what will people say? Do you know how many people look up to us? You're so selfish."

We ate the rest of our meal in silence. No matter how often I tried to get a response out of him, he refused to talk. He looked like a man just enjoying his food, but I knew better, and I instantly regretted everything I had said to him. The weeks following my birthday lunch were the same. Mark only spoke to me when absolutely necessary but avoided interacting with me the majority of the time. It was as if I ceased to exist in his book.

He left his phone open on Facebook one day while he took a shower and I scrolled through only to find sexual exchanges between him and multiple women in his inbox. Something in my gut told me he had been cheating on me for years, but I never entertained those thoughts, and now the proof was staring me in the face.

I knew something was coming. I could feel it in my gut he would get revenge because that was how it had always been. If he was unhappy with something I said or did, he would always exact revenge. But I knew his infidelity was not the revenge because that was nothing new. Soon time would tell.

10

LIGHTS, CAMERA, ACTION

I received an email one day from a television producer named Kyle with a Hollywood production company asking to set up a meeting with me. Apparently, they had seen some viral social media videos and heard about a few of us in the community competing in rodeos, which sparked a special interest in us. They were also intrigued that an acquaintance and I started a business, Urban Cowgirls, LLC, to inject equine education in the black community as well as promote emotional and mental wellness through equine activities, so they set up a video meeting so we could tell them more about ourselves.

Surprisingly, the producer, Kyle, was very friendly. He was listening intently and asking all the right questions, such as how we started and what our community was like and so on. It was great talking to someone who was so enthusiastic about something so close to my heart... until he asked me personal questions.

"So, I hear you've been married for over 20 years," Kyle said. "Does your husband share your passion for horses?"

"Not quite," I laughed nervously. "But he supports anything that makes me happy."

"Couple goals," he clapped happily. "I think it would be great to show people that such a great love exists. You know it's hard to find the real thing these days."

"I guess I got lucky," I laughed.

"Absolutely! You have someone to grow old with," he smiled.

Suddenly, the room began to spin. My heart raced like crazy and black spots filled my vision.

"Charlie? Charlie... are you ok?" I could faintly hear Kyle call out to me after a long pause when I failed to reply.

"Uh, I...I'd like to excuse myself for a moment to get some water. I was in the sun working the horses earlier and feel a little dehydrated."

Breathe, Charlie. It's going to be ok, just breathe. I

told myself while in the kitchen pouring a glass of water.

I returned within moments with a big smile plastered on my face, sat in my seat in front of the laptop to continue the video meeting and with a deep sigh I said, "Now where were we?"

"What would you say is the glue that has held your marriage together?" Kyle continued his questioning.

"I would say the secret to any relationship is honesty and respect. We always have each other's back," I replied confidently.

"That's true," he mused. "Add respect to anything and you've got a winner!"

"R. E. S. P. E. C. T.!" I playfully sang the famous song by Aretha Franklin.

He went on asking in-depth questions about my relationship that would be normal for an interview, but to me, it was eye-opening. Hearing the lies coming out of my mouth about how supposedly amazing my relationship was, opened my eyes to more than I could have imagined. I had been living a lie for over two decades, but the real question was, what was I going to do about it?

The producer told me one of the casting directors would be in touch with me and after that meeting, we would discuss the way forward. This news should have been exciting, but all I could think was if this opportunity manifested, Mark would only sabotage it.

Who knew all it took to bring about some serious introspection was a single conversation with a stranger?

~

A filming crew was sent out to film a sizzle reel a few weeks later, and I was over the moon. Being on TV wasn't something I'd ever sought, but it was an exciting opportunity and I felt cowgirls- especially black cowgirls- needed more recognition and representation so it was an honor to be the one who could potentially open new doors for my fellow women in the community. The crew filmed at my house because it was very spacious with great scenery, especially for the intro-packages.

"Excuse me ma'am," a tall and handsome caramel toned man with a camera approached me. "We need a few shots of you in front of your house."

I put my iced tea down and followed him and the makeup artist to the front side of the house.

"Zack is an amazing photographer," the

makeup artist, Jazmine, whispered as she touched up my makeup. "And girl ain't he fine? I hear he's single," she added. "Should I make a move? I'm going to make a move... Maybe I shouldn't. What if he's not attracted to me? I can't do it!" She continued to freak out.

"I'm kind of old fashion and probably not the best person to get dating advice from," I responded and left her to get my photos taken.

"I see you're a Bears fan," I remarked when I noticed the emblem on Zack's baseball cap.

"Yep, I'm from Chi-Town," he replied with a smile on his face as he changed his camera lens.

"Aw man, you must be gutted about losing to the Packers AGAIN," I quipped.

"Yeah, yeah, we have the better offensive line though." He shrugged.

"And yet you ate dust," I chuckled.

We went back and forth for a few minutes and then he asked me to pose in front of my house. He was so meticulous with how he wanted to capture the visuals. I was thoroughly impressed by his work. We shared personal stories and laughed over the next day as if we had always known one another. He seemed like the kind of guy I could be friends with because he was easy going. We shared similar interests, but I was not someone who crossed boundaries.

At last, we were done with the photoshoot. All that was left to do was film the rodeo competition the next day in which I was a contestant.

I was so excited I went to bed early that night so I could wake up ahead of time and do a couple of beauty treatments in preparation. However, in the wee hours of the night, I heard my youngest son screaming for help. Little did I know I'd end up in the emergency room, with a broken wrist because of Mark. To cover up as I was accustomed to, I told the police in the ER I fell down the stairs.

As soon as Mark and I returned home from the hospital, I got out of the car bewildered by the chaos and retreated to my room. I got into bed with hopes of going to sleep and no longer living this nightmare. Mark didn't come inside. Instead, he drove off in search of Junior.

I struggled to undress with the use of one arm, so I just sat there collecting my thoughts and mind mapping how to unfasten my bra. A few moments later, I was startled by the incessant loud banging on the front door. With one hand, I frantically grabbed my robe, draped it over the temporary cast, and made my way to the bedroom window. To my surprise, there was a police car parked in our front yard.

My heart sank into a pit of despair and an uncomfortable knot formed in my stomach. I grabbed my cell phone and secured it between my knees and texted Mark.

Me: The police are at the door, what do I tell them? Truth?

Mark: I'll be there in a minute.

I made my way down the stairs, sweating profusely, and the sound of my heartbeat echoed in my ears out of nervousness. I composed myself and opened the door to face the police officer. He looked directly at my arm in cast held with a sling looked past me as if to gauge if anyone else was there before questioning me.

"Are you ok?" he asked. "Your son, Mark junior, requested we do a wellness check on you. He told us you may be in danger."

There I was, torn between telling the truth after I lied and said I fell down the stairs to the police in the emergency room. As I stood there about to take the lifeline thrown to me by the police officer and regurgitate everything had just transpired hours prior, Mark strode up the walkway and greeted the police officer with a warm smile on his face.

"Hey Officer, come on in out of this rain." Mark welcomed the officer into our home and struck up a conversation with him.

He told a fake story about how he had to show his son some tough love hoping to keep him out of the streets. Now, everyone knew Junior was a gentle giant. He was a very respectful young man who displayed a calm and quiet disposition. This passionate story about "tough love" was Mark's way appealing to the officer as a concerned father. Mark was charismatic and very convincing. He was so persuasive he could get people to do what he wanted or see things his way.

I watched as the police officer negated the fact I was standing before him in a cast and empathized with Mark's story about tough love and how difficult it is to rear responsible young men. I had once again witnessed how well Mark could manipulate people. At that point I turned to the stairwell and ascended to my room, leaving them to enjoy their casual banter.

Although I was in pain, I managed to pull out my laptop with my working arm began to search the internet for answers. Over the years, Mark was so emotionally detached and unapologetic. There was a myriad of search results, but one stuck out to me because I remembered briefly learning about it in one of my psychology classes back in college.

"Narcissistic Personality Disorder? Could this be it?" I mused. When I saw the traits of a person with NPD it turned out to be the perfect description of Mark's behavior.

My eyes had been opened to the truth. At first, I didn't understand why that nightmare had come up again after so many years, but I was glad I was reminded of my childhood because now it made me desperate to get out. That nightmare made me realize all the work I had put in to not be in an abusive relationship was in vain because I had been in one all along, but now I was awakened. I just had to figure out how to manifest the freedom I could now picture in my mind.

11

PLOTTING AND PLANNING

The plan was simple. Become the perfect wife while planning inconspicuously.

Having lived with Mark for over 20 years now, I knew the only way to escape was to play by his rules. He was so good at mind games, so I knew I had to be very alert and strategic, but at the same time, careful.

I was paranoid about writing in my journal, so I created a secret document in one of my work folders on my computer. The document was so well hidden no one would find it, even if they went snooping unless they were interested in federal fiscal policies.

Becoming the perfect wife meant stroking Mark's ego until he let down his guard, I prepared myself to be submissive and acquiescent to everything he wanted, including satiating his large sexual appetite. But first, I was starting with breakfast in bed.

I prepared a stack of home-made pancakes with warm syrup, bacon, scrambled eggs, and freshly squeezed juice. My hands were trembling as I approached the bedroom door. This went against my nature, so the physical effects of the psychological change were taking its toll on me. I took a few minutes to calm down and plastered a fake smile on my face before I walked in.

"Good morning, baby," I greeted him cheerfully.

Mark sat up in the bed, eyeing me suspiciously. "What's all this for? What are you trying to do?"

I put the tray on his lap and sat next to him, sighing dramatically to support my acting. "Well, I had a little heart to heart with Bianca... "

"She got a man?" he interjected.

"Yes Mark, she's married remember!" I gritted my teeth but kept the smile on my face.

"Good," Mark mumbled as he wolfed down the food, "Them single bitches are a bad influence on you."

"You're right," I agreed, even though my tongue was burning with a retort. "Bianca sat me down and made me realize I wasn't being a good wife to you so I'm trying to change."

"See, that's what I've been saying, though," he nodded vehemently. "That Bianca chic has the right idea."

"Yeah," I winced, but Mark missed it because he was engulfed by his meal he didn't notice. "She made me see the light."

Mark practically swallowed his meal whole and immediately turned his attention to me. He started kissing my shoulder while telling me how happy he was I was becoming a good wife and I had to remind myself not to shudder at his touch because he disgusted me.

My mind kept reflecting on Dr. Raine's advice about proper planning to ensure better odds at post-divorce success. It was now time to improve my credit score, save money, sell my rental property, research places to live and find a good divorce attorney.

What added an extra layer to my research was I was convinced Mark was a narcissist. Narcissists view their partners/victims as objects to be owned, controlled, mistreated and used as emotional punching bags; not as individuals of free will and leech off of their compliance. They become addicts to this type of control they gain in relationships which is deemed as narcissistic supply. Once the victim escapes and they no longer have access to their resources (financial, physical and emotional) which provide social proof of their normalcy, they become enraged and hell-bent on wheels to seek revenge. Therefore, I knew leaving him would bear major consequences.

I did all of my research on my work computer and made calls from my work phone. No one was privy to my plans, not even my girlfriends. It could have been paranoia, but I just couldn't risk any information somehow getting back to Mark.

After all, as the saying goes, "your closest ally can be your worse adversary."

~

My days all began to look the same. They started with breakfast in bed for Mark followed by sex, after which I'd take an extra-long shower scrubbing myself down to cleanse myself of him and reminding myself it would all be over soon. From there I would drop Junior off at school and head to work. My day would wrap up with horse chores followed by a lavish dinner. Steak, lobster and shrimp which were among his favorites.

"You're filing for divorce?" Bianca shrieked.

I was so engrossed in my business conversation on the phone I didn't hear or see Bianca peeking over my shoulder. She had flown into BWI airport which was near my job and wanted to surprise me. She looked bewildered as I frantically closed all my tabs.

"Calm down!" I whispered and prayed no one heard her.

Bianca's panic-stricken face worried me. "Charlie, what is going on?"

"Look, you can't tell anybody okay?" I begged her. "Please B, I need you to keep this to yourself."

"Not until you tell me what's going on," she said defiantly, even though I knew she wouldn't tell a soul.

"I can't talk here," I told her. "But please just trust me."

"My place, tonight," she ordered with her no-nonsense voice. "I'm going to gather the girls. I've never seen you this terrified, Charlie. Whatever it is, you need to let us help you."

"But I-"

"7 pm," she interrupted and got up to leave. "Don't be late."

My months of planning secretly had possibly gone down the drain. I didn't know what to do. I had full confidence in my girls, but anyone could slip up. It was human nature to make mistakes.

I called Mark and fed him a bullshit story about Bianca wanting to see me so she could call me out on my behavior of not being such a good wife so I wouldn't be home for dinner. He was ecstatic just hearing someone was "calling me out" that he didn't question it. The rest of the day was a blur because I was worried about how much to tell my girls.

When I walked into Bianca's house later that evening I found I was the last to arrive, which was unusual. I read the worry on their faces as soon as they laid eyes on me and instantly knew I was going to tell them everything. They made assumptions about my marriage over the years, but I always covered up. They were used to the easygoing, take-charge, I can do it all Charlie; not the fragile, paranoid, mentally defeated Charlie whom I had been hiding from them for years.

"I don't know where to begin," I chuckled dryly.

"Right at the beginning boo," Anthony spoke for the group.

"Hell," I exhaled slowly and took a seat. "My life has been a living hell. I thought I married a wonderful man. I thought I'd have a different marriage to the one my parents had when I was younger. I thought my mother was weak all those years, and I swore I'd never become like her. Can you believe I didn't even realize I was being abused?"

That night, I told my girls everything. I told them about how manipulative, egotistical, self-centered, entitled, verbally, emotionally and physically abusive Mark had been. I told them everything from his excessive affection and attention initially to the heartless man he became shortly after we got married. I told them about my multiple miscarriages and how Mark only seemed to care about me when I was pregnant or sick. I told them about the affairs he had and how he'd wake me up in the middle of the night to smell my underwear, saying he felt like I was cheating on him. I told them about his verbal attacks that would last hours on end and sometimes the whole night and the truth about the night he broke my wrist. I emptied myself of all the toxicity I had endured in my marriage, and they listened and cried with me.

"So, you're not only divorcing him, you're escaping," Raquel said intuitively.

"Yeah," I shrugged. "I have to. There's no other way."

"How can we help?" Crystal asked.

"Y'all don't have to do anything," I shook my head. "I've got this."

"Yeah, that's a NO from me, dawg," Anthony piped up. "We're going to help you whether you like it or not, so deal with it."

"What Anthony said," Bianca added. "Wait, Mark knows about the divorce?"

"Kind of," I nodded. "I first brought it up on my birthday, but I've officially filed now."

"And he's cool with it?" Raquel asked.

"Well, he thinks I want to work things out, I decided to play the role of the perfect wife to buy me time while plotting my escape," I replied. "I worked on getting my credit in order, researching investment options, and how to build a life after divorce."

"You go, girl!" Bianca high-fived me. "That right there is a boss woman!"

I finally saw the real me in the mirror. The chains were breaking off of me one by one and with each fallen link I discovered a part of me I didn't know existed. I finally believed in myself and in the truth I had to fight for myself because I was worth fighting for.

As soon as I played Mark's game all the fighting stopped. I could tell he had forgotten all about me wanting a divorce because of how sweet

I had become. I became very calculated as though it was a game of chess. One wrong move and I knew he'd take me out. The newfound peace in our home was what I had longed for all the years we were married, but now I could see peace was costly and came at the expense of ME.

12

THE BUBBLE BURSTS

We planned a group trip to the Essence Festival in New Orleans and I knew in my heart this would be one of my final good memories with Mark. A few other couples came along, including my sister Michelle even though her husband couldn't make it due to his new job.

The expectation for all of us was high that this would be a trip to remember. We went to all the tourist restaurants, attended concerts, laughed, and danced all night long and everyone was having the best time... except for me. I kept a smile on my face and tried to participate in the various activities as much as I could so no one would notice, but I was emotionally exhausted. Catering to Mark by letting him have his way physically, emotionally and financially began to take its toll on me.

I spent the majority of my time trying to over-compensate and appease Mark to stroke his ego and make sure he was having a great time to not spark his attitude. I diverted everyone's attention when we went to restaurants and he would order two or three meals because he couldn't choose and I'd foot the bill. He loved to indulge in food and overeat, but if I tried to say anything or stop him, he would cause a scene, which is what I wanted to avoid at all costs.

During one outing as a group on Canal Street amongst the huge Essence Festival crowd, we stopped at a cigar shop and looked around. Mark bought a cigar and gave me his phone so I could take a picture of him pretending to smoke it.

"Fire it up!" Michelle encouraged him.

Bianca, and I joined Michelle in edging Mark to light up the cigar. We were chanting and making funny gestures to hype him up in good fun.

"Make the pic official Babe! We're in New Orleans, so go for it!" I encouraged him.

"Yeah, Mark! Make it official!" Bianca added.

As we laughed and tried to get him to light it up, I noticed his expression slowly changing. I covered it up by buying a cigar and doing silly poses to distract the girls, and thankfully it worked. However, Mark acted like a completed ass for the rest of the trip. He wouldn't walk by my side or speak to me, so I had to act a little "extra" to cover up his mood so no one else would notice. There were even times when he would be on his phone talking excessively and posting pics on social media as if he were alone. When the gang engaged in small talk he made it a point tune the entire group out. It was as though he found humor in watching me cover up his childish antics.

Just as we all were scheduling our shared rides to depart Canal Street, I looked around for Mark to confirm the next stop on our itinerary and he was nowhere to be found.

"Charlie, where'd Mark go?" Michelle asked me with a grimacing frown.

"You guys can go ahead, I'll be fine. Mark went to get us some beignet's to take back to our room for a late night snack," I lied convincingly.

Everyone hopped in their shared rides one by one and departed off to their next destination. I stood there, holding back my tears, as they drove off. It was a familiar sad and lonely feeling.

Everything in me wanted to hop in an Uber to go to our hotel for my belongings and get on the next flight to DC. I was tired of being mistreated. However, the curiosity in me wanted to know where Mark disappeared to and what explanation he would give once he surfaced.

I looked around to find a spot so I could stand off to the side out of the busy crowd. As a distraction, while I waited, I pulled out my phone to surf social media. To my surprise there were pending unopened messages.

Message from Unknown Woman: Hey sexy! I see you're in NOLA. Why didn't you take me with you?

Mark: Hey beautiful! I just needed to clear my mind and get away. Besides, I also had some business to tend to out this way. I'm gonna hit you up when I get back.

Message from Unknown Woman: This is what you have waiting for you when you return (caption of inserted nude pic)

While reading the messages, my hands shook uncontrollably and my throat closed off as though I just suffered a peanut allergy.

A couple years prior, I started social media accounts for Mark and I. At that time, the passwords created were identical for us both. We never changed it. So when I would go into social media, I had the option of choosing his profile or mine. The messages I read were under Mark's messenger account. The crazy thing was Mark knew I had the password and he never changed it. It was like he got a thrill out of knowing he was cheating in my face.

Out of nowhere Mark surfaced and asked where everyone went as if he hadn't disappeared for over 30 minutes. When I inquired where he'd been, he said he was in a karaoke bar a couple doors down admiring their sound equipment. I didn't even mention the messages because I didn't have the mental headspace to deal with his classic gaslighting. His famous line was social media was just for shits and giggles. It was all make believe and I needed to stop being insecure.

Within moments, our Uber ride pulled up and we hopped in. Although Mark had a chip on his shoulder, he opened my door as a gentleman should but that was merely for public display. The ride back to our hotel was utterly silent. When we returned to our room he immediately turned on me and accused me of making a mockery of him. He said I was down right disrespectful and didn't know my place as a woman. He also went on to say I sought out to purposely embarrass him to impress some guy in the crowd. As usual, I was too exhausted to defend myself, so I apologized and went to get ready for bed. That night, I laid awake and replayed those Facebook messages in my mind over and over. Surprisingly, I did't she one tear. I was numb.

Mark thought he defeated me once again. Little did he know, this time the fiery woman in me was fed up and ready to take back control of her life, and this was the final straw.

~

"I filed for divorce," I told Mark a few days after we got back from New Orleans.

"Bitch, I been done with you anyway. You just beat me to the punch that's all," he responded.

Judging by his reaction when I told him I had filed for divorce, he had not taken my words that night at dinner seriously. The countless times I told him I was unhappy or that I would file for divorce if we didn't work on our marriage seemed to have flown over his head, and now I was seeing a completely different side of him and I don't think any amount of preparation could have prepared me for what came next.

"Get the fuck out dude!"

Mark was yelling at the top of his lungs, throwing my belongings on the floor and trampling on them. He claimed the master bedroom, even though the mortgage loan was solely in my name. Instead of having a civil conversation like a normal person, he was cussing me out and throwing a fit like a 2 year old trapped in an adult body.

"Mark, stop," I begged him. "I'll move into the guest room, just stop, please."

"Bro, stop harassing me! Get the fuck out the way!" he said as he pushed me aside out of his path.

"What are you talking about? I'm not harassing you," I countered. Clearly, I wasn't harassing him. This was just another one of his gaslighting tactics.

I looked at the clothes, shoes, jewelry, memorabilia, etc. sprawled around the room which perfectly paralleled the chaos in my life. There was no reasoning with Mark. He wasn't the kind of person who listened, neither did he take opposition very well, but I kept trying to make peace with him. It didn't make sense to have strife with a person I was married to for 25 years.

A couple weeks later, I received a $38,000 bill from an IRS audit. I knew right then and there a war had begun and Mark was going to fight dirty and he would stop at nothing.

13

MAGIC CITY

Zack: Happy Birthday!
Me: OMG...You remembered.
Zack: How have you been?
I was surprised when I received a text from him on my birthday. It was so special he remembered or noted it in his calendar. I was so elated to hear from him. I thought about him often and reflected on how refreshing our conversations were. He seemed like a good person from the couple days I spent working with him. What I didn't see happening was the friendship that sprouted from our mutual love of football.

Ever since I was young, I always got along with guys better. Maybe it was my tomboyish nature or the fact I spent so much time working with my dad it was easier to make male friends because all the things I enjoyed were typically male-related; sports, horses, cars and politics. I was easily one of the guys.

Zack and I started to text back and forth about random things and I looked forward to his texts. I updated him how Mark and I's marriage took a turn for the worse and I filed for divorce. Not once did I come clean about how tumultuous my divorce had become while talking to him. Something about him made me want to protect the friendship from the toxicity in my life; almost as though it was my safe haven, so I wanted to keep it pure. Our friendship was strictly platonic. It was like a breath of fresh air. For once, other than my girls, he was someone who appreciated me for me with no strings attached.

Anthony invited me on a trip to Atlanta. I accepted without hesitation. It was a great opportunity to get some much-needed space from my situation, and it would also give me the chance to see my sister since we didn't see much of each other now she lived in Atlanta.

Michelle and Anthony had larger-than-life

personalities, so I knew spending some time with them would help me forget my troubles.

I sat in the passenger seat and watched out the window as we passed couples walking along our way. I reflected on how I had spent over half of my life with Mark. Memories crept in on my desire to build a life and family together. The thought of walking away from that was very difficult, but it was necessary. I had now come to understand commitment was not in words but action. Everything Mark had promised when we met and when we got married had given me the promise of a great life with a great man, but his actions heavily contradicted his words.

"Nah uh, we're not doing that this weekend honey," Anthony scolded me as he snapped his fingers loudly in my face as I looked out the window.

"Doing what?" I asked him.

"The spacing out shit and feeling sorry for yourself," Michelle answered from the backseat.

"Sorry," I smiled. I couldn't even argue with them because it was true.

"We're getting turnt tonight! We are hitting the strip club missy so you can brush up on your moves since you will be single soon." Anthony said animatedly with his tongue pointed to reach the bridge of his nose.

Within seconds, we pulled into a seedy-looking strip mall. Some of the businesses had lighted storefront signage that was missing a letter or two. Litter adorned the curb alongside the parking space we pulled into. And there it was before us, the infamous Magic City strip club. I nervously got out of the car not knowing what to expect. I never been to a strip club before, so I was intrigued.

At the club entrance was a long line of people waiting to be checked for weapons upon entering the establishment. The three of us took to the rear of the line. Anthony took this time as his opportunity to adjust my clothing to be more befitting for the occasion.

"Yasss, Bitch! That's more like it," he said as he unbuttoned my blouse just above my naval. "Now, let's get in here and take notes."

As we entered the establishment, the mood was set by the loud Trap music with X-rated lyrics. My senses were immediately assaulted by thick smoke from marijuana, hooka and cigars. Throughout the club, there was a sea of beautiful nude women of all sizes with small waists highlighted by the roundest derrière Georgia peach. Their bodies were all shades of brown imaginable. Body oils glistened off their skin with an array of neon colors from the strobe lights above. Some seductively danced on poles while displaying the most acrobatic competency skills. Others performed hypnotic movements as they straddled their adorning customers fulfilling their sexual fantasies. Dollar bills decorated the stained carpet. Men were off to the side shooting pool, drinking beer and taking shots while others were just lounging, eating wings and ordering food from naked waitresses wearing 5-inch pumps.

While Anthony and Michelle tucked dollar bills in the dancer's G-strings I watched on in amazement admiring the women's bodies. Their silhouettes and flexibility were mesmerizing. I didn't feel the urge to judge. Instead, I took it all in and felt free to be unbridled. All I wanted was to lose myself in that moment and give in to the music and seductive atmosphere.

As I watched the hypnotic movements of the dancers, my mind went straight to Zach. I imagined his hands and lips roaming my body. All types of crazy fantasies flooded my mind. My nipples began to tighten and my honeypot started to pulsate. The wetness that followed soaked my cotton thongs. I was ripened and ready for picking. If only Zack was here and knew how I felt.

"Oh my God! You're burning up!" Michelle exclaimed after mistakenly brushing her hand along my cheek when she was getting up.

"Maybe we should get some air," Anthony suggested.

"No, no, I'm fine!" I told them. "I just need a drink with lots of ice, please."

"I'm on it!" Anthony offered with a quick flip of his wrist.

We stayed in the strip club soaking it all in until the break of dawn and spent the rest of the day resting up because Anthony and I would be driving back to Maryland the next day.

Anthony had me in stitches on the drive back.

"So," Anthony popped his lips, "You take a Fruit Roll-Up and line it on the roof of your mouth, but you gotta be discreet about it because no man wants to see someone eating candy before giving head, it's all about the surprise, hunty. Oh yeah, don't suck on it otherwise it dissolves. So, when you put his dick in your mouth, the Fruit Roll-Up wraps around it and ...boom! Magic!"

I listened attentively while fantasizing about trying it out on Zach someday. Anthony was our sex guru; his advice never failed, so I never doubted him. None of us knew exactly how he discovered these crazy tips he always gave us.

Later that night after Anthony dropped me off, I tiptoed through the house so I wouldn't wake Mark or Junior up. Even though Mark and I were sleeping in separate bedrooms and living separate lives, I didn't want to give him any more ammunition to use against me. He was always ready to pick a fight, so I didn't want him to ruin my good mood.

I stopped dead in my tracks when I heard Mark's booming laughter coming from his bedroom. "That raggedy whore thinks she's all that," he said and toppled over laughing.

Mark was on the phone with someone whom I assumed was one of his friends, judging by how he was freely expressing himself. He never let his "gentleman" mask slip unless he was talking to someone in his inner-circle who knew who he really was.

"I'm telling you, man," he replied to the person he was talking too. "Oh, you don't believe me? Nigga, I give you a pass to try and fuck that hoe. That bitch will spread her legs like an eagle," he continued to laugh hysterically.

14

STEAMY GRITS AND BISCUITS

Zack: What are you up to?

Me: Getting my nails done. I can't pick a color though.

Zack: I think powder pink would look great on you.

Me: Really?

Zack: Hold up, let me send you a picture.

He sent me a picture a few seconds later of a beautiful set of powder pink nails with an intricate abstract design. I showed it to the nail tech, who gushed about "my man" and I didn't correct her.

Zackary became my best friend in every sense of the word. We spent hours on the phone every day for months now, talking about everything and nothing, and just enjoying each other's company.

He made me feel safe. He supported and encouraged me more than anyone else; always ready to lend an ear. But most of all, he treated me with the utmost respect. He taught me how to love and respect myself, and to accept nothing less from those around me.

It was because of Zack I understood I didn't have to be with a man to have value as a woman. I finally understood I didn't need to be Mrs. Somebody to be validated.

~

My cousin Eryka called me one day and told me about a major event she was hosting. The moment she told me where it was being held, my mind went straight to Zackary. Truth be told, I had been looking for a reason to visit LA so I could see him, and my cousin just gave me that reason like an angel sent from heaven.

"I'm hosting in LA," my cousin, Eryka, told me.

"LA?" I asked with a little too much enthusiasm. The event she was hosting in LA was called, "Grits & Biscuits," which was a traveling DJ set. My ears perked up the moment she mentioned LA, and my body trembled in excitement.

Zack and I lived on opposite coasts so the only time we had physically seen each other was when we first met, so this was the perfect opportunity to see him again.

"I'd love to come!" I told my cousin.

"Are you serious? That'd be great!" she replied, equally excited. We hadn't seen each other in a while, so she was happy I'd be able to come.

I immediately booked my flight and hotel when we hung up and told my sister and my girl-friends I'd be flying to LA for the weekend. Naturally, Anthony and Raquel wanted to tag along, but I shut that down real quick! I wanted all the time I could get with Zack so I couldn't have anyone else around.

In preparation for my upcoming trip, I took a day off to get myself together in every way possible. I'm talking body scrub, full-body Brazilian wax, Manicure, Pedicure, the whole nine yards. My confidence was also through the roof because I had been working out like crazy to make myself feel better ever since I filed for divorce.

My stomach was knotted a million ways when I arrived at the airport on Thursday morning, but this resulted from my uncontrollable giddiness as opposed to my fear of flying. I felt like I was high on something because I could not contain the joy bubbling within me. This was the first time I had ever traveled anywhere other than to see family by myself. Actually, this was the first time I had done anything alone.

"Will your partner be joining you?" the concierge asked me when I arrived at the hotel.

"Nope," I replied with a big smile on my face. "It's just me."

I realized in that moment I was free to do whatever I wanted. I didn't have to compromise or ask for permission; I could literally go wherever I wanted, eat whatever I wanted, and do whatever I wanted, and the only person I had to answer to was myself. It was then I truly felt the next chapter of my life would be okay.

I entered my hotel room and approached the window to take in the spectacular view of the city. The sight of passerby's had me lost in thought until I suddenly realized to call Zack. I anxiously pulled my phone out of my pocket and plopped down on the bed with arms spread eagle wide. Al-

though we talked every day, I was so busy preparing for my trip I hadn't spoken to him before
my departure.

I was nervous about seeing him. A tiny part of
me— a minuscule part— wanted to back out as
my insecurities crept in.

"I'm about to make your day," I teased as soon
as he answered.

"Make my day," he replied right away.

"I'm here! I'm in your backyard," I chuckled.

"Wait, you're in LA?" he asked.

I caught him up on the details of my flight experience and joked about how I wouldn't be getting any use of the bikini I packed since LA was
unseasonably cold when I arrived. As we talked, a
text message came in from my cousin.

**Eryka: I missed my flight so I won't be there
until tomorrow evening shortly before the show.**

**Me: No worries. I'll find something to do. I'll
go sightseeing or something. Don't worry about
me. See you tomorrow night at the Palladium.**

Unforeseen change of plans gave me the opportunity to do something bold.

"Hey, I know we made plans to meet tomorrow,
but how about you come by the hotel to meet me
tonight when you get off work?" I asked.

"Sure, I'll call you when I'm on the way," he replied.

Meanwhile, for the rest of the evening, all I could think about was finally seeing Zack.

Like a true gentleman, Zack called and said he would wait for me in the hotel lobby, which was great, but the thing is, I was full-on trying to seduce the man because I was in love with him and I couldn't hold it in any longer. I wasn't sure he felt the same way about me, but it was a risk I was willing to take. Due to his line of work, Zack was always around gorgeous women and in my mind they were my competition and so I felt I had to show him I could be more than a friend to him.

Zack called me and asked why I was taking so long, but little did he know, I was trying to shift our friendship to a romantic sphere. I often wondered why he wasn't making the move and if he only saw me as "one of the boys," so I took it upon myself to make the move and find out once and for all. I asked him to come up to my room and waited for him with bated breath.

My heart nearly jumped out of my throat when I heard a knock on the door. There was no turning back now. Even if I wanted to back out, how was I going to explain the dimmed lights, rose petals, and wine? Plus the fact I was wearing next to nothing.

I shook my fear off and took a few deep breaths before slowly opening the door and peaking around it. I may not have been the most attractive woman he had ever met, but I was determined to leave a lasting impression. I zoned out, going over my strategy in my mind so I wouldn't miss a step and ruin everything.

"You good?" Zack's rich, sultry voice sent shivers down my spine, and I was positive he wasn't doing it on purpose, or maybe it only sounded sultry to my ears.

I unlocked the door and turned away as I waited for him to enter. He slowly pushed the door open when I wouldn't say a word and strode into the room in his usual confident manner. My back was turned to him, but I could feel his eyes on me and suddenly I felt overwhelmingly vulnerable.

I stood before Zack in a sheer black robe with satin Polka dot trimmings that fully exposed my black lace bra and matching thong with tassels and watched him as his eyes traveled the length of my 5ft 9in frame body. I had never seduced a man before, so I went with my first instinct and attacked him with a passionate kiss. My mind was focused on doing everything I possibly could to ensure I satisfied him because that was what I was accustomed to, but then he pulled away from me.

My heart sank as the familiar pangs of rejection and disappointment crept in, but then he gently wrapped his arms around my waist ever so delicately and we locked eyes. My breath hitched in my throat when I saw the desire in his eyes, and it only made my heart race faster.

He backed me up against the wall, pinned my hands to the wall with his and kissed me gently on the forehead, and then he slowly moved down and kissed me on the bridge of my nose, and with a thoughtful rhythmic seduction he softly traced the outline of my lips with his tongue, and then he kissed me deeply but ever so gently. He caressed me like I was precious, valuable, but not fragile.

His kiss alone was far better than every sexual experience I had ever had, and the proof was in the wetness between my legs. He stopped kissing me and looked into my eyes once again. He didn't have to tell me he loved me because I knew it from that very moment.

And then he picked me up and led us to the bedroom where he set me down at the foot of the bed and took his shirt off. "Oh... my... God," I exclaimed in my already breathless state. Zack was ripped! His abs looked like puzzle pieces that were locked together! I knew he was a fitness enthusiast but seeing him up close like that blew my mind.

I was so busy ogling him I didn't realize he had stripped down until he turned me around and traced the length of my neck with his lips. His lips moved with gentle precision from my neck and down my spine while slowly taking my robe off simultaneously. My eyes rolled back in my head and I let out a soft moan as he tasted every part of my body.

He got down on his knees and hooked a finger into my thong and slowly took it off, leaving a trail of kisses wherever the fabric touched. We locked eyes again, and I gave him a slight nod, then he picked me up and wrapped my legs around his neck. I arched my back as he peppered my vagina with kisses, and then his tongue did what I can only describe as magic.

That night, I had planned to seduce him and thought of all sorts of tricks and positions to please him, but instead, he ended up pleasing me.

When he was done, he pushed me further along the bed and positioned himself between my legs and kissed me deeply as he slowly entered me. I gasped when I felt the full length of his swollen manhood inside me. It was like a thousand butterflies were released in me. Zack completely intoxicated me with passion, and I couldn't get enough. He looked at me lovingly and kissed away each tear that escaped my eyes. I didn't even realize I was crying until he kissed my tears away.

Our bodies moved in perfect synchrony as we made love, bursting at the seams in ecstasy. We kept going until we were both fully satisfied, and then he led me to the shower where he insisted on washing me, but it was as though he was memorizing every part of my body with the way his hands roamed over me. I stood there as if he was the artist and I was his muse.

But what really surprised me was he put the toilet seat down. To someone else, this was something trivial, but it was a big deal to me. In all my years being married to Mark, he had never put the seat down; not once.

I looked at the time when we got back into bed and saw we had been making love for over two hours. It was certainly the longest sexual encounter I'd ever had, and also the most passionate. I always thought sex was about pleasing a man, but Zack showed me it was supposed to be pleasurable for me too, but most important, I deserved it.

"What are we?" I asked Zack when we woke

later. "I'm 45 now, definitely too old to be someone's fling."

"Charlie," he replied calmly. "You're still legally married."

"But my divorce will be finalized in 30 days," I countered. "I'm ready for a relationship."

Zack sat up and took both my hands in his. "I don't think you're emotionally equipped to make that decision for yourself right now," he said while gently rubbing my hands.

"You've been through a lot Charlie," he continued. "I want you to make healthy decisions. I want that for you because I love you. You've been a mother and a wife your whole adult life. You need time to figure out who you are and what you really want and that takes time."

"I know I want you," I replied stubbornly.

"Charlie," he sighed. That was another thing I loved about him. He wasn't into the whole calling your partner "babe" as everyone else did. He believed saying the person's name communicated he recognized them.

"I want you in my life no matter what," he reassured me.

"Even if I fall in love with someone else?" I asked.

"No matter what," he repeated, and then he sealed the conversation with a kiss.

❧

Zack drove me to the airport on Sunday and noticed I was acting guarded. I did my best to hide it, but he knew me so well. We said our goodbyes and my insecurities had flared up. I reverted to feeling like I wasn't good enough.

When I got on the plane, I wrote out a long-winded text to him in which I thanked him for being such a great friend, but I drafted it in such a way it sounded like we'd never see each other again. It wasn't even a full minute after I hit send my phone rang and his name flashed on the screen.

I watched it ring repeatedly on my lap until he gave up. My whole being was itching to hear his voice, but my ego wouldn't allow me to. I picked up my phone, intending to turn it off when the screen suddenly lit up, showing me I had a text message.

Zack: Are you ignoring me?

Me: Sorry, I'm a little busy right now.

Truth be told, I had never been too busy for Zack in the months we had known each other. We had always prioritized communication, so we never ignored one another. Also, it was a terrible lie given I was on a plane.

Zack: Are you mad at me?

Me: Why would I be mad?

Zack: Please answer your phone?

"I'm not mad," I answered coldly when he called again.

"Charlie, you need to work on your relationship skills!" he replied, sounding genuinely frustrated and confused.

"Excuse me?" I replied with an attitude. I was ready to defend myself as I had done for over two decades with Mark.

"*Listen* to me. I need you in my life. Just because we can't start something right now doesn't mean anything is going to change." he said kindly.

It stunned me to silence. I didn't expect Zack to fight for me, much less put up with my insecurities. I was self-sabotaging thinking I wasn't good enough for him, but even though he continually validated me.

"I'm sorry," I said, feeling embarrassed and defeated.

"It's okay," he sighed. "Just don't shut me out, okay? I don't want to lose you."

My experience with Zack was more than just

sex. Zack got to know me for who I was, not the Charlie who had been mentally broken down over two decades, not the Charlie who had lost her confidence and self-love because she had been abused. No! Zack saw the real me, and he cared about me enough to help me reconnect with that woman.

15

THE BEAST UNLEASHED

"I'm not signing off on the mutual consent divorce unless you sell the rental property and give me 50%," Mark said one day.

"What are you talking about?" I frowned.

"The rental property," he clarified. "Are you a retard? What part don't you understand? I want my cut. And I want it now!"

I probably had an "if looks could kill," moment because his demand, was ludicrous.

"Are you serious, Mark?" I asked him. "I worked myself to the bone to buy that house and when I asked you to chip in you flat out said 'no.' Not once in the entire 15 years of me owning that house have you helped out with maintenance or responded to complaints from the tenant."

"Either I get what's mine or you're going to have some serious problems," he threatened. "Try me, hoe."

I will not lie. I was angry. The rental property was not only an investment, but it was my pride and joy because it reminded me I could do anything I set my mind to in spite of the obstacles. That property was the reason I could afford to send Nathan to private school since Mark refused to pay for anything concerning him. Mark treated Nathan like trash until he was ranked #1 in the state for his football position and scouted by over 20 division 1 college programs. Only then did Mark become father of the year, telling everyone how much he invested in our son when in reality; I was the one paying for everything and attended high school football games alone.

The rental property meant a lot to me. Each time I went to see the tenant I'd look around and remember how I managed every aspect of it single-handed and made financial sacrifices just to afford the renovations and repairs over the years. It was my baby, and Mark was taking that away from me too.

The day of the sale was torturous for me. I understood, by law, he was entitled to something. But 50% for someone who contributed 0% over the years was ludicrous. I made a regretful mistake 5 years prior when I refinanced to pay off our joint debt as well as his $17,000 truck balance and put Mark's name on the loan. He abused his financial position to get his demands met.

Mark was giddy all morning due to the fat check he was about to receive, and that only infuriated me. He had finally agreed on getting a little lower than 50% because I told him I had to pay off the IRS (he bought it), but I would not have peace splitting the proceeds down the middle with him for something I worked so hard for alone.

"So how would you like the proceeds to be divided?" the attorney asked once the sale was complete.

"50/50," Mark replied immediately with the biggest grin on his face. I watched him salivate over this money for weeks now, and I couldn't take it anymore.

"That was not our agreement," I spoke up, which surprised him.

"Don't mess with my money, Charlie," he warned in a calm voice, but I knew it was meant to scare me. Unfortunately for him, I was tired of being bullied.

I calmly stood up, thanked the attorney for his time, and then I turned to face Mark.

"Well, the money can sit in escrow for all I care, but over my dead body will I give you 50%."

With that, I picked up my bag and walked out. Mark thought I was bluffing at first, but he quickly realized money didn't mean much to me, so he gave in after a couple of days... and thus my opportunity appeared.

I drafted a letter stating he would get 47% of the proceeds from the sale of the rental property, but I took it a step further and wrote the actual amount he would receive in dollars. True to form, the moment Mark saw the dollar amount it intoxicated him. I could see the lust in his eyes, and I prayed it stayed that way because if he read the rest of the document he would find out that by signing it he was agreeing to the divorce being mutual and immediate as well as having to live in the primary home splitting the bills until one of us moved out, in which case the remaining party would be liable for all costs of the house.

As expected, Mark only cared about the large sum of money and agreed to sign the document in the presence of a notary as per my request. The moment the letter was signed and notarized, I immediately emailed it to my lawyer, who then shared it with Mark's.

"You ugly ass nigga!" Mark went off as soon as I answered the call.

"You signed it, Mark," I replied calmly. "You had plenty of time to read it."

"Fuck you, stupid bitch ass hoe! I'm gonna make you pay for this you grimmy nigga," was his vulgar response. I was so used to this kind of language and behavior it didn't faze me this time, so I ended the call.

I sat in the car looking at my reflection in the rearview mirror and then screamed at the top of my lungs, overcome with relief and excitement. I rolled down my window and screamed out to the world, "I bought my freedom!"

After Mark received his share of the money from the sale of the rental property, he went wild. He started bringing prostitutes over to our house, going on lavish vacations to Thailand, Dubai, Los Angeles, and Las Vegas. As if that wasn't enough, he went on a $25,000 shopping spree and flaunted all this on social media. He was acting like a total fool.

He completely lost control, spending money like a madman. Mark splurged on a $4,000 cologne collection; Creed, Prada, Gucci, and other high-end brands. He gorged himself at expensive restaurants every night and went out with his friends more than usual, and always bragged he footed the bill.

As much as it hurt to see him waste my blood, sweat, and tears, it was a small price to pay for my freedom. Unlike Mark, money was never my biggest priority because I valued peace and love over it, so I let it go and thanked God I was done with Mark, hopefully for good.

～

During this time, Nathan packed up and moved to Los Angeles to get a fresh start. This inspired me to consider California as an excellent place to reinvest the proceeds from the sale of my rental property since he had been struggling to get on his feet, he would at least have stable accommodation before I put it out on the market for rent or resale.

After feverishly looking online, I found a property and put in an offer to purchase without ever stepping foot in the home. It was a perilous choice, but my father taught me never to second guess my gut instinct. I went for it and lo-and-behold it turned out the property was inhabitable and needed serious renovations, which sounded like good news to my ears because that meant I had a new project to divert all my energy into.

Admittedly, I wasn't happy about the extra money I now had to spend on renovations, but I felt blessed because it gave me a solid distraction from all the madness going on with the divorce. Due to the nature of the renovations, I had to fly to Los Angeles almost every other week to stay on top of everything, which meant all the time I spent there was time less spent being around Mark.

By some miracle, Junior got a job at an airline that gave him free flights as an employee, so I never had to pay for my flights to LA. Everything was aligning for my benefit. My prayers had been answered.

❦

"Here," Mark said smugly as he tossed a document at me.

"What's this?" I asked him, but he remained silent.

I read through the contents of the document a couple of times, but it was not making sense to me. Mark presented me with papers he paid his attorney to draft which stated if I ever returned to our home, I would be reported for fraudulently purchasing a house, but the thing is, what he threatened to do was not legal, and I was shocked his attorney had gone along with it.

"Is it even possible to fraudulently purchase a home, Mark?" I asked him incredulously.

"Nigga, you think you're so smart, but I smarter," he snickered.

I sighed and got up to leave. "I don't have time for your games," I told him. "I have a flight to catch."

Mark stood in front of the door and went off. He was yelling expletives, per his usual, but I stood my ground and fired back. It became apparent the only way to get my freedom was to fight head-on for it. When Mark realized I would not back down he turned to leave, but at the last second he looked back at me and said, "If you return, I will be sure to make you vanish," and he stormed out.

His words sent chills down my spine, and for the first time I truly feared for my life. The more I uncovered this side of him the more I realized I was dealing with something dangerous and if I didn't get out, there would come a point where I wouldn't get out alive.

I refused to give him the satisfaction of seeing

me tremble in fear because it seemed like he fed off of it, so I kept a straight face and rushed to the airport to catch my flight.

~

Mark: **Please stop harassing me. I'm scared for my life.**

I read Mark's text message as soon as I landed and couldn't believe my eyes. He kept creating these false narratives via text and email, but in person he would say things like, "I'm going to make you pay for all of this," and threaten to have me arrested and lose my job.

Instead of feeling excitement about renovating my property, I was now filled with anxious thoughts of what Mark could be planning for me next. I was so afraid I thought he was setting me up to shoot me when I got an alert notification from my door camera and saw a video of Mark having the locks changed.

Upon my return to Maryland, I immediately went to the courthouse and asked for a protective order, which was granted immediately.

Not one to be "outdone" Mark immediately sought a protective order against me in retaliation.

"She said she was going to have me dealt with,"

Mark's voice trembled while making a statement under oath. We both had to show up in court to plead our cases because the protective orders were only valid for 72 hours, and I watched in disbelief as Mark lied to the judge yet again.

The judge dismissed both our cases and asked us to talk things through like adults, which in theory was the best thing to do, but Mark was far from rational. When they let us out of court, he rushed to his car and sped away.

Thankfully, the judge confirmed if I broke the locks to enter the home I'd be within legal rights because it was my home, so I called Anthony and asked him to help me gain access.

Bianca and Crystal were in court with me so they witnessed everything. They finally understood just how malicious and vindictive Mark was so they refused to let me go home alone just in case he did something crazy.

Anthony broke through the back door with a crowbar and none of us were prepared for the sight before us. It looked like a tornado had passed through the house. Mark had destroyed 80% of my clothes as well as memorabilia and scattered them everywhere. Clothes were strewn all over the floor, on the kitchen counters, in the living room, on the dining room table; it was a complete mess.

We were all lost for words, but Bianca looked the most upset. "Grab what you can. You're staying at my place tonight," she said, and then headed for the guest room, assumedly to help me pack a bag.

~

As the weeks followed, I stayed between Bianca's place and my house with Mark whenever I was not in California working on the investment property. Whenever I was at my house in Maryland, it was absolute hell. Mark acted as though I didn't exist, and it tortured me mentally. He stopped talking and would brush by me as if I was invincible if we ran into each other in the hallway. What made everything worse was he told people I no longer lived there. I'd walk in on him on the phone telling someone I moved out months ago.

The longer this went on, the more I questioned my existence and my sanity. He'd say things like, "I haven't seen that woman for months. She's probably off fucking someone for money," while I was sitting across the room from him.

He would then bring random women in the house and leave them parading around half-naked when he went to work, and from the looks of it he told them to pretend I didn't exist. All these random people were coming in and out of my home acting like I wasn't there.

Just when I thought it couldn't get any worse, I received a call from the cops telling me theft charges were filed against me and I needed to go to the station as soon as possible to be serve my notice to appear in court. This was a serious accusation, so I immediately got off work and rushed to the station to find out what was going on.

"Ma'am," the officer sighed, "I understand divorces can get messy, but stealing isn't the way to go."

"I didn't steal anything," I countered.

"Well, it's either you prove it or you will have to compensate your husband," the officer shrugged. "And listen, I think it's best you stay off the property like you agreed."

"What do you mean? I live there? In fact, the house is in my name," I frowned.

"Ma'am, your husband said you moved out months ago when the divorce was finalized. Look, I don't know who's telling the truth, but all I'm going to say to you is that it's not worth it," the officer replied. I could tell he pitied me, and I hated that. I didn't want to be pitied, I wanted to be vindicated.

I drove home feeling frustrated and confused. Mark had accused me of stealing $20,000 worth of his clothes, which was ridiculous. Although we were getting divorced, we had agreed to share our home until everything was finalized, which began to feel like a big mistake.

When I got home, I searched the entire house until I found the clothes Mark had accused me of stealing. He had hidden them in a Louis Vuitton suitcase in the garage. I pulled out my phone and took pictures as evidence and even sent them to my attorney and Junior as proof.

I sat in front of my vanity mirror that night, just staring at my reflection. It was as though my existence was slowly being erased and I was losing a grip of reality. I pulled out my fuchia lipstick from the vanity drawer and wrote on the mirror.

"Charlie... lives... here," I softly read out the words I had written on the mirror.

I had developed memory loss, irritable bowel syndrome, extreme anxiety, insomnia, and chest pains that mimicked a heart attack; that was all stress-induced. My eyes looked empty, detached from the world. I felt as though I was neither living nor existing, which was both confusing and ter-rifying.

"Charlie... lives... here," I repeated, hoping the sound of my voice would raise my conviction.

Right at that moment, Mark burst through the door shouting about something. From his reflection in the mirror, I saw he stopped dead in his tracks, but the real horror was not his presence but the look on his face. The corners of his mouth slowly turned up in the familiar evil smile I had seen too often. He walked towards me and slowly bent down until he was at eye level with me. "You think you're crazy now? You ain't seen nothing yet. I'll show you crazy. Mess with me and you will leave this house in a body bag." And with that, he walked out.

16

THE CAKE CAPER

Each of the girls as well as Anthony had given me a key to their homes. They were adamant about me not returning to my house in Maryland with Mark. Everyone was concerned for my safety. Sadly, I was so numb to Mark's threats after a couple of weeks passed, I returned to the guest room in my home in Maryland. After all, it was my house as well. I had every right to stay in it per our agreement. To make matters worse, Mark refused to pay his share of the mortgage. Since partial payments are not accepted, the loan was now several months behind. Any attempts to have him sign the release to list the house for sale were to no avail. His response was "My name ain't on the house so this ain't my problem."

~

Bianca made plans for the 5 of us to hang out at her house for the night. However, Anthony and Raquel couldn't make it. They both had dates that night.

When Crystal and I arrived, Bianca was drooling over the fresh batch of cookies her neighbor just delivered.

My face lit up when I received a text message from Zack.

Zack: Knock-knock.

Me: Who's there?

Zack: Nobel.

Me: Nobel who?

Zack: Nobel... that's why I knocked.

I burst out laughing. Zack would text me random jokes throughout the day as his way of letting me know he was thinking of me.

The three of us were sitting on the living room carpet snacking on cookies and telling embarrassing stories when I remembered something important and had the overwhelming urge to share it.

I blurted out, "Mark's cousin makes the most amazing Jamaican rum cake!"

Crystal crouched down and suspiciously whispered, "I want Jamaican rum cake," as though it was a secret.

Bianca looked around and gestured for us to huddle and put our heads together and she too whispered, "I've got a plan, but you can't tell anybody."

"One of us should call her and order the cake using a fake name," Bianca continued in a hushed tone.

"You should do it. You're smart," I giggled.

Crystal supported my idea and Bianca called Mark's cousin under the pseudonym Liza Bennett. I don't know how we came up with that name, but when Bianca called and introduced herself as "Liza" it had us in stitches.

Placing the cake order had gone perfectly. We were so proud of ourselves until Mark's cousin called back and asked to change the delivery location and time.

"Oh my God, I think she knows!" Bianca placed her cell phone on mute and whispered in full-blown panic.

"What are we going to do?" I asked, panicked as well.

Crystal mouthed the words, "Corner... strip... mall," in what should have been a whisper but turned out to be the opposite. Bianca relayed the new proposed location and Mark's cousin agreed. Now we were good to go.

When we arrived at the strip mall, Crystal and I shrunk down in the backseat as far as we could go, completely oblivious to the fact Bianca's car had tinted windows. We snickered as we watched Bianca, concealed in a black ball cap with a wide brim and oversized Aztec sweater, sprint back to the car with a white cake box decorated with a gold bow in hand.

"Code 3! Code 3! Mission accomplished!" Bianca whisper-yelled when she got back into the car and sped off toward her house.

We were so paranoid, but at the same time so amused with the situation we couldn't stop laughing. We laughed at every silly little thing we saw, and the laughter continued when we arrived back at Bianca's house and went back to our spots on her living room floor and devoured the cake. None of us had anywhere else to be so we slept on the floor.

The shrill ringing of Bianca's phone awakened the three of us the following morning. She was still a little out of it, so she put the call on loud-speaker.

"I'm so sorry, Bianca," Judy, her neighbor, apologized.

"Um... I forgive you?" Bianca answered groggily.

"I gave you the wrong batch of cookies yester-day," Judy confessed.

"It's fine Judy, the batch you gave us was lovely so I'm not complaining," Bianca replied.

"You don't understand," Judy stressed. "I gave you edibles."

The three of us stared at each other in shock for a few seconds, and then we burst into laughter. No wonder we did said such crazy things the night before, we were high as kites!

At least for one day I didn't think about Mark, his pending theft charges against me, the past due mortgage payments he refused to pay or the fact I was pretty much living house to house. I focused solely on having a good time and it turned out to be better than expected, but I had to return to my reality sooner or later.

∾

17

TRUSTING THE UNIVERSE

"This is called a lantern release," Raquel explained.

Instead of our usual picnic, she asked us to do something different because we were in the first moon phase which is the manifesting phase. We were sitting on a hill overlooking the city, each with a pen, paper, and a lantern.

"I'm going to lead you through some mantras, and then I want you to write what you want to manifest on your piece of paper, put it in the lantern, then we will all release them together."

We moved a bit further apart for privacy as we meditated and wrote what we wanted to manifest. My paper was empty though. I knew what I wanted most, but I was afraid to put it down on paper. "True authentic love of self and others," I whispered to myself as my pen hovered above the paper.

I wanted true love most.

My phone buzzing in my pocket startled me because I thought I had turned it off. We weren't supposed to be on our phones as per Raquel's instruction, so we would have no distractions, but I was too curious to wait so I angled my body away from the group and placed my phone under my thigh so they wouldn't see the light from my screen.

Zack: "Love yourself enough to take the actions required for your happiness. Enough to cut yourself loose from the drama-filled past. Enough to set a high standard for relationships. Enough to feed your mind and body in a healthy manner. Enough to forgive yourself. Enough to move on."— Steve **Marble**

I don't know how he did it, but Zack was always in tune with what I needed. It was as though an invisible tether connected us no matter how far apart we were. We had a deep spiritual connection.

"Charlie, are you ready?" Crystal asked from behind me.

"Almost," I replied, suddenly having the courage to put to paper what my soul needed.

True love. Write a book. Generational wealth.

These were the three things I wanted more than anything else. I chose to blindly trust the universe and have faith everything would fall into place regardless of how messy things were going.

I got up and joined my friends, and the five of us lit the wicks and released our lanterns into the sky. It was a beautiful sight watching them float up and away. It seemed like they were headed straight for the heavens.

"Trust the universe," Raquel's soothing voice broke the silence. "When we trust the universe, we turn into unicorns!"

The rest of us giggled because it sounded so ridiculous, but the serious look on Raquel's face quickly shut us up.

"I'm serious, y'all," she protested. "When you genuinely surrender and accept yourself for who you are; when you truly own that, and surrender yourself to God, the possibilities are endless."

I wondered what my life would be like if I surrendered myself like my lantern floating in the sky, and let the universe guide me, and right then I decided to just surrender myself and find out. I had nothing left to lose.

~

As I laid in the bed, I looked at the security bar I had propped below the door handle as means of security in case Mark was to burst in and try to harm me. It set in my mind that I was playing with fire and at the expense of my life. I had been staying in Maryland because that was where I worked. But now, a worldwide pandemic had hit and my job issued mandatory telework orders. Right then and there I decided I would move to the other side of the country. My motivation was to get as far away from him as possible, so he would have no means to torment me any longer.

Just as I turned to switch off my bedside lamp, I noticed a picture sticking out of one of my drawers. Sadness washed over me as I recalled the day the picture was taken. No matter what we said or did, there was no way we would get back to that place.

Looking at each person's smiling face broke my heart. I believed my dysfunctional marriage was only affecting Mark and me, but now I knew just how many people it affected and it finally sunk in, life would never be the same. I realized some of these relationships had been severed by Mark and I's divorce, and that hurt even more.

Mark and I were no longer legally tied to one another, but I still wanted the best for him. It was sad it had ended in such a vile way. Everybody chose a side, and the majority was on his. But that didn't bother me, I just wished it didn't have to be that way.

I pulled out my phone, snapped the picture, and attached it in an email to Mark, and then I wrote:

The picture below brought back many memories of two motivated kids with good intentions and a bright future. All I could think of was how EVERYONE in the pic has been ill-affected by the toxicity in our relationship. More important, our children have been forever changed.

In a world with so much beauty and love, how did I end up in a relationship that lacked each one? Tears, hatred, guilt, blame, anger, resentment. We both inflicted emotional pain, verbal and hateful words, and an unapologetic lifestyle. I guess all we both ever wanted was for each to look into our soul, feel our tears, feel our pain.

I'm not perfect. I never will be. I lied. I hid things. I shut down to avoid you. I said things to make you feel the pain I experience instead of what I truly felt. I didn't trust you like you didn't trust me, and that doesn't sustain a marriage. But I loved being a wife, and I loved the idea of you; what you once were to me when we first met, what I thought you could be, or the idea of everything I dreamed we could be. It's undeniable, at our best we were one hell of a team.

Our marriage is now over. Here we are post-divorce and still hurting each other, and people around us are standing by for the grand finale. I'm tired of looking like a spectacle. I'm not asking to be friends, carry on conversations, or go hang out. I'm just asking ... can we for once be HUMAN to one another?

Our past reflected the vibrational pull we each emitted, and I take full responsibility for my share. I understand now I am the center of my own universe and have control over what I attract. I choose peace in my life and a healthy mental wellbeing. Hence why I am sending this letter in sincerity to stop the fighting, disrespect, and elevate to a higher frequency and treat one another as humans.

Out of this all, the best thing we can do is teach our kids to vibrate high and create the life they want by being the energy they want to attract.

I want to end by saying I truly loved you. Thank you for the years, the children, the good and the bad memories. I genuinely wish you all the happiness I could not provide.

Peace & Warmest Regards,
Charlie

Barely a few minutes went by and my phone lit up, signaling a new message from Mark. I had a glimmer of hope thinking I had gotten through to him, and then I read the message and accepted there was no hope.

Mark: Please stop harassing me. I'm scared for my life right now.

18

APRIL FOOL'S DAY

Chaos! The world was in absolute chaos. Everyone was panic-stricken as the country was being locked down due to a world-wide pandemic, the Coronavirus. It was spreading like wildfire and taking lives. The world was gripped by fear and forced to shelter in place, but to me, this was the little glimmer of hope I needed to finally make my escape. My girls helped me plan the perfect escape. All that was left to do was wait for Mark to go to work.

I got up early to get ready. I could not afford to waste even a minute after Mark left for work. I took a quick shower and changed into a black t-shirt, military-style cargo pants, a black baseball cap and black sneakers. One would think I was going to war with the way I was dressed and in a sense, it felt like it. I was fighting for my freedom.

After getting dressed and doing some last-minute packing, I slowly opened my door and peeked into the empty hallway. I briskly tiptoed to my son's room for a last-minute attempt to convince him to come with me. Truthfully, I knew what his answer would be, and I understood his reasoning, but I still had to try. He was old enough now to make his own decisions, but I felt uneasy leaving him alone with his father, especially since the incident left him with a damaged shoulder.

I lightly knocked on Junior's door, hoping he would be awake. He was aware of my plans and in full support. No matter how hard I tried to convince him to move with me, he remained firm in his decision to stay behind because of his job and girlfriend. There was nothing I could do about it because he was now a young man, so the only thing I could do was support his decisions as he'd done with mine.

Junior was sitting at his desk working on something when I walked into his room. My girls had been staking the house, waiting for Mark to leave so we could move the furniture. I had left my room the moment I heard Mark shut the front door, so I only had a few minutes alone with Junior before it was game time.

"I'm sorry, Junior," I told him sincerely.

"Stop apologizing, Ma. None of us have had it easy with Dad, but you and Nathan had the courage to leave and I'm proud of you," he said.

"You can come with me. You don't have to go through this anymore," I pleaded with him.

"Don't worry about me, Mom," he smiled sadly. "I'll be alright."

Those were disappointing words to hear yet again, but I had to respect his wishes, and I also had to get moving. Bianca texted to let me know they had seen Mark drive off and they were at the front door.

We only had 4 hours to get everything done and hit the road before Mark came home. Because of the Coronavirus lockdown, he only worked 4-hour days, so we had to execute our plan swiftly. Not only were we taking half of the furniture, which I thought was fair, but we also had to load the horses, so there was no room for mistakes or hesitation.

Junior got up and hugged me and then walked downstairs with me to give us a hand with the furniture. With the extra pair of hands, we had everything loaded in 3 hours and 45 minutes, which meant we had to leave immediately.

We split up into two trucks. Bianca and Anthony had the horse trailer hooked to their truck, and Raquel, Crystal, and I followed behind them with the furniture in tow. Anthony hooked up a radio device to both trucks so we could talk to each other on the way, which worked great when we started with our karaoke.

Thus we began the 7-day-long journey to California. Bianca was the most traveled out of all of us and she loved planning things, so she had taken it upon herself to map out the route we were going to take and all the stops we'd make along the way. I was both grateful and impressed when I saw how much time and research she put into it, considering she was a very busy woman.

As the buildings turned to fields of grass, I looked at my friends and smiled. "I'm free," I laughed with tears in my eyes, "I can't believe it's over."

"You did it, sista!" Raquel cheered from the backseat.

Crystal didn't take her eyes off the road, but she cheered along with Raquel. "Drinks on me at our first stop!" Anthony added over the radio.

"Can we have champagne?" Bianca asked, and we erupted in laughter.

Nothing can compare to that moment when we left the city. A part of me wanted to cry because I was leaving decades of memories behind. I'd always thought I would retire and grow old in Maryland, but I never would have imagined someday I'd be packing up and moving across the country to get away from a man I once loved.

Pound by pound, the weight was lifted off my shoulders with every passing mile. I was taking a leap of faith into the unknown, fully aware there was no turning back. Deep down I knew my move was not about my son- Nathan- or Zackary, who I hoped to have a future with; it was about me and freeing the woman in me who had been bound by oppression.

The hustle and bustle of the city turned to the peaceful stillness of nature, and my anxious heart began to beat in synchrony with the dancing of the flowers to the music of the light spring breeze. It was only when my Junior texted to tell me Mark returned home from work in a fit of rage, I noticed the date: April 1st, 2020.

"April fool's day," I chuckled dryly.

"Well damn, that's right on point," Raquel added.

"The Irony," Crystal laughed.

To me, it was a sign from the universe I had made the right decision. It was a sign my life was coming into alignment and it felt good. I was truly free.

~

Our first stop was in Columbus. We had been on the road for almost 8 hours, so everyone desperately needed rest. Generally, the drive should have taken about six and a half hours, but we had to drive slower and more cautiously for the sake of my horses. Anthony strictly warned us to stay on schedule because we had animals with us, so we couldn't go overboard visiting all the great tourist spots along the way, plus we were dealing with a global pandemic, After much begging, however, he agreed to let us do at least one tourist activity at each stop.

"To Charlie!" Crystal raised her glass after giving a heartfelt speech.

"To Charlie!" everyone cheered and clinked their glasses together.

We were having dinner at Melt Bar and Grill because it had vegan options, but mostly because we'd heard they had amazing cocktails. If it were up to Anthony, we would have gotten wasted celebrating my new life, but we enforced the 3-drink maximum rule which we had created years back at an event when one of us, I won't say who, got a little too "happy" with the drinks. Well, that rule did not apply at trail ride after parties, in the club, or when we had girl's night.

Bianca the drill sergeant woke us all up the next morning and rushed us to get ready so we could stay on schedule. After a quick breakfast we were back on the road, but this time Bianca and I switched, so Anthony and I were in the first truck with the horses and the rest of the ladies were in the second truck with the furniture.

It was a bit of a struggle leading the horses back into the trailer before we continued our journey. It broke my heart because I could feel how anxious they were, and the unfortunate truth was we had a few more days to go before arriving at our final destination. I was thankful for Anthony's presence because he was more skilled in handling them as a professional horse trainer, especially when they got antsy.

Oklahoma City! That's where the true adventure would begin. From Ohio, we drove through Indiana, Illinois, and Missouri before we finally got to Oklahoma- the beginning of all the fun.

"Okay ladies," Bianca snapped her fingers, "We're halfway to our destination, which means it's time for a little fun."

We were having drinks at a bar in Oklahoma City that was emptier than usual due to the pandemic. Apparently, each state had imposed different guidelines for the pandemic. The only guidelines that were consistent were face coverings, modified business hours and reduced maximum capacity of business establishments.

"Our dear Charlie gets to do the honors by going first," Bianca continued. "Your first dare, is to seduce a man... without touching him."

"Woooh girl! You better tantalize all his sexual chakras," Raquel cheered me on.

"Mmm, and I just found your target," Anthony moaned sexually. "Tall, chocolate, and packing at 6 O'clock."

I peeked over at the guy Anthony mentioned and he was indeed cute and easy to spot since the place was damn near empty, "Okay, okay, so what are the rules?" I asked.

"You have five minutes to make him get a hard on," Crystal popped her lips. "You've got to make him stand up so we can see that print."

"Remember, no touching," Bianca added.

I took a shot of tequila first because everyone

needs some liquid courage in such situations and walked up to the man. He was much more handsome up close from what I can tell that wasn't covered by his face mask, and judging by his loosened tie and grim eye expression, he'd had a rough day at work.

I perched into the seat next to him at the imposed 6ft distance and turned on the charm, "What's a handsome man like you doing at a bar all by himself?"

He chuckled in amusement, put his glass on the counter, and turned to face me, "Are you trying to pick me up?"

"Isn't that the line men use most of the time?" I smiled. "Hi, I'm Lexi." Rule number one was to never give out your real name.

"Kevin," he said as he extended his elbow for a mutual elbow bump to be COVID safe.

I looked over Kevin's shoulder and my friends were all waving their arms and shaking their heads for me not to touch him, so I gently flipped my hair and unbuttoned my top a little to distract him.

"That's not the kind of touching I prefer," I told him seductively.

Anthony almost ruined my game face because he was making all sorts of dramatic faces and fanning himself. If Kevin turned around, he would see how dramatic Anthony was being and it would ruin my dare, so I tried to keep his attention on me.

"Hmm, I see," Kevin rubbed his chin. "Tell me more about your preferences."

When his eyes drifted down to my cleavage, I knew he had taken the bait; I just had to get him to stand up so my girls could see the proof. I got up seductively, which encouraged him to stand up as well. He must have thought we were going somewhere private. When Anthony, who was close by, verified Kevin was aroused, he gave me a thumbs up.

"That's classified," I smirked. "It was nice meeting you, Kevin."

I left Kevin standing there with his jaw dropped and walked back to my girls who were all asking what I said. Before I could even say anything Anthony gave them the full play-by-play with extra spice because he was dramatic like that.

"Well damn mama," Raquel high-fived me. "You still got it."

∽

The next few days on the road were filled with laughter and drama. Raquel taught us some advanced yoga poses she did during sex for maximum pleasure. We had to stop in a little, barely populated town called Black Rock in New Mexico because we had been on the road for over 10 hours. Now, Black Rock didn't really have much going on so we stayed indoors for the night. Crystal called us all into her room saying she had an emergency, when she was bored and wanted company.

Never one to miss a moment, Anthony took the "stage" and educated us on the right way to give a man head. First, he began by telling us all the locations he had done it in before, as well as the pros and cons of each, and then the demonstration began.

"Y'all heffers telling me none of you brought a vibrator?" he shook his head in disappointment. "Have I taught you nothing?"

"I'm married," Bianca giggled.

"Bitch please, everybody's got one," Crystal laughed.

"Me and mine get acquainted quite often," Raquel added.

"Fine," Anthony sighed dramatically. "Pass me that hairbrush."

We all sat up and paid attention as Anthony launched into the first detailed scenario of where this might happen— the bedroom. After a step-by-step tutorial with the hairbrush and a few personal stories thrown in there, Anthony exhaled as though he was exhausted, "... "Just to recap, don't choke it with your hand, it's not wrestling. Don't whip out your veneers and graze it, just no, okay. And lastly, exercise that tongue ladies. Any questions?"

"What if it's too big?" Crystal asked.

"Uh-uh, ain't no such thing," Raquel snorted.

We tried our best not to laugh too loudly because we were at an inn and the owner was right downstairs, plus the walls were very thin. .

I made sure everyone was asleep, and then I got up and went outside to have a moment to myself. We were having so much fun on the trip there were moments I forgot what was really happening, and I needed to process it all.

"It's surreal, right?" Raquel's voice startled me.

"I thought you were asleep," I replied.

"It's a full moon tonight," she said while pointing at the sky. I looked up and indeed it was.

"I made the right decision, right?" I asked her. "It's not crazy I randomly decided to move across the country, right?"

Raquel sat beside me and put her arm around me. "Charlie," she began solemnly, "The universe brought everything into alignment and opened the door you had been looking for all these years. All you had to do was walk through it and you did. You have the right to peace."

Our late-night made us hit the road a little later than we had planned the following day. Our girl chat was fun, but what stayed with me was the moment I had with Raquel while everyone was asleep. Her words had given me the courage to embrace what I didn't realize I deserved all these years: peace.

~

"Next stop, The Grand Canyon," Bianca announced over our radio as we were driving through Arkansas.

"That wasn't part of the itinerary," Crystal replied.

"Trust me, it's necessary," Anthony added, and then he and Bianca stopped talking.

Crystal and I looked confused, but Raquel seemed peaceful, as if she was in on it. We had all been to The Grand Canyon before, and Anthony was very strict about his schedules, so I knew something was definitely up.

"This will be the true beginning to your healing," Raquel said as the five of us stood watching the breathtaking view. "What you're going to do right now is scream at the top of your lungs." She instructed me.

"I don't think so," I chuckled nervously. "You guys know how I am."

"Exactly," Crystal gently rubbed my back. "We brought you here so you could break free of all these limitations. You've gone through so much over the years and you've been keeping it all in."

"You were in on this too?" I asked Crystal, remembering how confused she looked when Bianca announced our brief detour.

Crystal's devious smile was all I needed to know. In fact, I should have known the four of them would pull something like this on me. Although I enjoyed having fun, I was very reserved where it came to expressing myself because I had been conditioned to stay silent so any conflict would end quickly.

Raquel gently nudged me forward while the rest of my friends stepped back to give me some space. Oddly enough, I felt a low heat rising in my chest and before I knew it I was screaming, crying, and yelling out expletives.

"I'm free!" I yelled at the top of my lungs. My tears of joy soon turned into uncontrollable laughter. I laughed so hard my ribs ached. My spirit was free, causing laughter to just bubble out of me uncontrollably.

My girls surrounded me and wrapped their arms around me while I laughed and cried. I was cocooned in a love so strong I knew nothing could ever hurt or break me ever again.

Years of gaslighting, manipulation, verbal abuse, sometimes physical abuse, all of that ended in that very moment. Mark no longer had power over me. He was no longer granted jurisdiction in my life, regardless of what he would do from that point on. At that moment, I took back authority over my life.

No words needed to be said when we got back into our vehicles and continued on our journey. The silence was exactly what I needed to process that my healing finally begun. The abuse I had witnessed in my parents' relationship in their younger years, and the abuse I had unknowingly been a victim to in my own marriage, all fell away. I was no longer defined by what happened. This time, I would create the life I knew I deserved. My mindset was completely transformed, and I would work hard to keep it that way.

19

THE CITY OF ANGELS

"Welcome to Los Angeles!" Anthony sang over the two-way radio a couple of hours later.

"We did it, girls!" Crystal clapped happily from the backseat.

"How do you feel, Charlie?" Raquel asked without taking her eyes off the road.

I shook my head as relief washed over me, "I can't believe we made it."

I felt like I was home. It's amazing how a change in environment can make all the difference. Although I was excited, my first thought was to call the stables I located for the horses and inform them we were nearby. I wanted to settle them as quickly as possible so they could adjust to their new environment. I found a place called Peacock Hill Ranch when I researched stables before our journey began.

I called the owner, Reese, and she told me I could bring the horses immediately because she was worried about the state they were in after traveling across the country, so I entered her address into the GPS and followed the directions until I arrived at a cast-iron gate with a big, round, red sign with the word "Welcome" written in bold letters.

The drive leading to the rustic farmhouse was breathtaking. A white picket fence lined the road and I could see people riding their horses at a distance and on the other side a few horses were freely grazing in the vast open field. Overall, it seemed like a very peaceful environment, which was exactly what my horses needed.

As soon as I excited the vehicle, my senses were intoxicated by an overwhelming scent of jasmine. The grounds were decorated by the most beautiful succulents of all kinds. A chic-looking woman, advanced in age, came out to greet me with a kind smile on her face. My first instinct was to be professional and polite, seeing as it was our first meeting, but she surprised me by wrapping her arms around me and pulling me in for a hug in spite of social distancing ordinances.

"Oh, my child, you look like you've been through so much," she rubbed my back and pulled away so she could take a good look at my face. "What's your story? Everybody here has a story."

She gestured to a group of posh women sitting on the deck with drinks in their hands, and only then did I notice them. Reese took my hand, my girls followed, and led us to the group. She introduce us to all of them.

The ladies organized a Margarita meet and greet night for me, which was so sweet. We all sat around a bonfire sharing stories about our lives and sipping on Margaritas. I was vague when they asked me about my life because I wasn't ready to talk about the life I had just escaped. I felt as though mentioning my ex-husband would taint my newly found peace and safe haven.

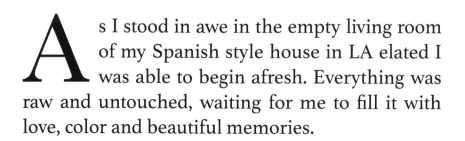

As I stood in awe in the empty living room of my Spanish style house in LA elated I was able to begin afresh. Everything was raw and untouched, waiting for me to fill it with love, color and beautiful memories.

As I sat next to the handcrafted primitive fireplace, I looked beyond the Spanish archways out to the backyard and noticed a vibrant sea of white climbing roses adorning the perimeters. All I could do was chuckle to myself. Mark made it a point to never buy me roses after we married. It was a form of punishment and another way to devalue me. Now, look at God! He gave me dozens upon dozens of roses to wake to, daily. That was confirmation nothing was stopping me from living the life I deserved.

My girls stayed behind at a nearby hotel because I needed time alone to soak it all in. Relief and excitement filled my chest and I took off running throughout the house. I was jumping, laughing and screaming because I succeeded; I was free to live my life on my own terms.

After 10 minutes, I was out of breath. I lay down on the hardwood floor and closed my eyes with a big smile on my face. My phone rang and startled me out of my dreamy-state.

"Hey beautiful," a smooth baritone voice echoed through the empty room. "How are you feeling?"

I loved that. Every time I spoke to Zack, I felt like he was caressing my heart.

"I feel... free," I told him. "I can't believe I'm free."

I had never been more at peace than I felt in that moment, lying on the dusty floor of my empty house. This new city coupled with my empty home was the blank easel I needed, and this time I would paint the best picture possible.

Zack and I spoke for a few minutes because he was on location shooting for a high-profile magazine. *And he still made time for me*, I mused after he ended the call.

It was like Zack had opened the floodgates because people started blowing up my phone after his call. My girls wanted to know when I would be back so we could grab a bite to eat.

I treated the girls to dinner since they would be flying back to Maryland the following day. I chose a restaurant in Burbank, The Castaway, with an amazing view of the city which would be appreciated since all restaurants were bound to outdoor dining. They came through for me when I needed them most and sacrificed their time to transport me and my horses across the country. They were friends that had become family, and I would be eternally grateful.

The crew were not emotional human beings, but I could see how hard it was for them to keep their emotions at bay during dinner. Even Bianca, who kept us laughing until our sides hurt, couldn't come up with anything to say. They were all trying so hard not to cry, especially because we were all eating silently with teary eyes and quivering lips. The excitement from the road trip had faded and left behind the reality we would now be separated.

Raquel cleared her throat and was the first to speak, "This is the end of an era," she smiled sadly. "I'm going to miss you, queen."

"Hey, we still have FaceTime," I chuckled lightly. "I'll become the Bianca of the group."

Bianca laughed and wiped a stray tear that escaped, "I should send you a bottle of champagne every time we have girl's night so you can flex on us." We all laughed because Bianca was always sipping on expensive champagne whenever she Face-Time'd us.

"I'll hold you to that," I told her. "I love y'all so much."

"We love you too," Crystal replied.

"Hey, at least we have a new vacay spot," Anthony added. "This is a good thing. I can't wait to taste the California cuisine."

I laughed and smacked his arm so he would stop ogling a cute guy who walked by our table, "You are something else."

We joked around about me getting into the dating world again because I was no longer hitched. Because they knew me so well, my friends quickly noticed I was avoiding anything to do with Mark. I deviated from any conversation that concerned him and saying his name was definitely off-limits.

That part of my life was one I wanted to forget. I didn't like the woman I was back then. None of those memories were welcome in LA. I didn't want him to have any more control over my life and talking about him would be giving him the power to control me all over again. There was no way I'd let that happen.

20

SNAKE OIL SALESMAN

Over the weeks, adjusting to life in California was not as difficult as I had anticipated. My only difficulty was not having my girls close by. Life was normal and quiet until one day I received a message that shocked me to my core.

I was casually drinking my coffee and browsing social media one afternoon when I noticed someone sent me a DM. Because I was focused on building my new life, I was cautious about people contacting me because Mark was very crafty and had already attempted to falsely file theft charges against me as well as accused me of threatening his life since I had moved to California.

Curiosity got the better of me, and I opened the message. To my surprise, it was from a woman claiming to know Mark. She sent me a long message that began with an apology. She explained she was introduced to him through his social media channel and they had intimate conversations after she commented on one of his videos and solicited him for counseling. I rolled my eyes when I read this thinking she was one of his agents sent to befriend me so he could receive information about me, but as I continued to read I got goosebumps and my heart raced as my mind was taken back to my horrific life with him. The woman told me he had bought her a plane ticket to Maryland to visit him. What was troubling, however, was after they had sex, all he talked about to her was me. She narrated how shocked and disgusted she was when they were done having sex, and he immediately began to curse me and reveal everything private he knew about me for two hours.

My first instinct was to not entertain this woman because I was in a good place and steadily healing from my past, but I just couldn't ignore it. I couldn't just sit back and let another woman fall prey to his schemes, especially after she said she felt abused because she contacted him for counseling and instead was coerced into a sexual encounter.

She realized the person he was on social media did not match the arrogant, boisterous, womanizer he was in real life. I blinked back the tears as I imagined what this young woman had gone through and how terrified she must have felt in that situation with him because I knew what that fear felt like. My vow to myself to completely cut Mark out of my life and act like he was dead had been a blessing to me, but now a curse to another woman.

My silence had caused another woman to get hurt. Still, I was trying to move on and heal from my traumatic past with him so I shrugged it off for the sake of my peace of mind, even though my conscience was saying otherwise. However, this only lasted a few weeks as I was contacted by yet another woman after leaving a comment on her social media page.

Now, after living with Mark for over 20 years, I had learned to be cautious of who I trusted. I knew how easy it was for people to misinterpret or twist my words to work against me, but there was something about this woman that felt genuine, so I took a chance and agreed to a phone call.

"So many women are reaching out to me,

saying Mark conducted himself inappropriately during their counseling session. One, in particular, said he was lying on the bed with the lights out during their counseling session via FaceTime and the more she cried, he seemed to get aroused and would seductively lick his lips. However, they are afraid to come forward in fear of retaliation by being also being targeted in his online smear campaign," she explained. "I too was in a relationship with a narcissist for many years, so I know all about narcissistic revenge."

"It just hurts me to see how many people he has deceived. All these men and women are under his spell."

Kierra paused and cleared her throat. "Uh, I have to ask," she said hesitantly.

"I'm not saying I don't believe you, but I need to see proof. I can't stand vile predators like him, but I can't go on my channel accusing someone without evidence in case he tries to sue. You have to be one step ahead of a narcissist. Mark has made some wild claims that can't be ignored."

"I haven't seen his videos. What claims are you talking about?"

"Well, he accused you of having an affair with your personal trainer as well as multiple men over the years, for starters. After that, he said you abandoned your son, which I assume is a result of you escaping. But he also said you were crazy and called 911 two hundred times making false claims. Not to mention, he claims you tried to get him arrested after you fell down the stairs and broke your wrist. These are serious allegations, Charlie."

I took a few deep breaths to keep myself calm. "The son he claims I abandoned is a 20-year old young man. His job and girlfriend are the reasons he refused to leave," I huffed. "Secondly, my personal trainer was gay... very gay. I've never had multiple affairs on Mark. Does he look like the type of guy that would let a woman run all over him like that? And I think anyone knows I would have been arrested had I called 911 over 200 times. Actually, I don't even think that's possible because the cops will arrest both parties when there are excessive domestic-related calls to an address."

"Wait... I thought your son was a little boy!" Kierra exclaimed in shock.

"Now you know how manipulative he is. Look, I've never done this before, but I'll send you proof so you can see all his accusations are false."

"Okay, okay, what about the whole deal about the house? He's always bragging about his massive house and you tried to mess up his finances. What's up with that?"

"Quite the opposite," I sighed. "That house he lives in, the loan is in my name only. He hasn't paid the mortgage since I left, even though he's the one who lives in it. He is behind by $60,000 last I checked."

"Aren't you worried the bank will repossess your house?"

"Honestly, Kierra, I've been begging them to take it. However, Covid-19 protection laws are preventing foreclosures. I just want this chapter of my life to come to an end. I'll show you proof of that as well."

We spoke for a little while longer and exchanged email addresses so I could send her documentation of what I told her. My heart raced as I hovered over the 'send' key. A part of me wanted to back out because it felt like I was opening closed wounds, but the wounds were still fresh and Mark's social media channel was nothing more than a smear campaign against me. Cyber bullying at its best.

I said a quick prayer, hit 'send,' and waited anxiously for her response. It's not that I needed her to believe me, but the validation I wasn't crazy or the narcissist Mark was accusing me of being, meant a lot to me.

Instead of emailing me as I expected, Kierra

called me back, apologizing profusely for what I been going through with Mark. She promised she would expose him, knowing fully the backlash she'd receive.

"Please don't reveal too much for the sake of my sons," I pleaded with her. "I don't want this to get any messier. They don't deserve to be caught up in this."

"But Charlie, they lived it too—"

"Not to the extent I did," I interjected. "They don't know everything and I want to keep it that way at least for now, until I figure out how I want to get the truth out."

Kierra was hellbent on exposing him, but she agreed to respect my decision. She created a video in which she exposed him and mentioned she had proof he was indeed the narcissist, but Mark retaliated just as she predicted.

When all these things happened, it was like something snapped within Mark. His retaliation was weird and psychotic. He created a 2-hour long video ranting and insulting Kierra and me and claiming I paid women to seduce him and make these claims. He said he had proof of his allegations against me, while shuffling some papers beside him, which he didn't produce. He literally gaslighted the viewers. Some of his followers noticed his weird behavior and called him out on it, but his followers were quick to attack these brave few viewers whose eyes had been opened.

Some people realized he was the narcissist, but sadly, the majority had already been brainwashed by his charming personality they could not see the truth about him. I knew this was a war would never end. He had been unmasked and his viewers were his supply. He would stop at nothing before letting anyone interfere with that.

As Mark posted his Live retaliation video against Kierra, viewers were demanding in the comments I come forward with proof. But I retreated and ignored their demands. It became quite apparent many could not care less about the truth or that Mark was using his social media channel as a vehicle to solicit and re-victimize women. Many wanted nothing more than a show and what I endured with Mark was traumatic and not to be minimized or circulated around on social media for entertainment or public opinion.

I called Kierra and thanked her for bravely calling out Narcissist life coach imposters and advocating on behalf of other survivors of narcissistic abuse, but this was a war I was tired fighting. She went on the tell me the narcissist wins by taking your voice. We continued on and I concluded I would speak out on my own terms and most important, when I was ready. The days of my actions being dictated by Mark were long gone. I was gonna take my power back my and redeem my character one day...my way.

~

Z ack invited me to join him and his girls for a picnic on a beautiful Saturday afternoon and I accepted. I had always been a lover of nature, but this time around I had a newfound appreciation for the clear blue sky, the birds chirping, seagulls flying, sounds of the waves crashing and the palm trees swaying slowly to the cool breeze.

I smiled at how sweet and caring they were as a family. It was easy to see how dearly the girls loved Zack. Watching them reminded me of the days my sons and I spent at the stables together when they were younger. There was such purity in the simple things in life that was unmatched.

Zack ran over to where I was sitting on a blanket on the sand with a notebook and pen in my hand. He nudged me playfully. "Charlie, Are you okay? Don't you want to come play with us?"

"I think I'll sit this one out. I'm finished with

the outline of my book," I shot him a smile. "Besides, watching the three of you having fun brings healing to my soul."

I could tell he understood exactly what I was saying by the way he looked at me. He kissed me on the cheek and jogged back to his daughters, leaving me feeling even more blessed than I had before.

Had someone told me a year ago I'd be living on the other side of the country and experiencing a pure and unselfish love, I would have said they were crazy. Who would have thought all those nights I cried myself to sleep, feeling afraid and trapped, would someday lead me to the beautiful life I had in front of me?

Leaving my home and not retaliating to Mark's smear campaigns had given me the freedom I had desperately sought for years, and it was worth it because I finally had peace. No assets or sums of money could ever be worth my peace of mind. Instead of hating Mark, I felt empathy for him. He was stuck and tormented in his delusional thoughts. He never moved forward because he was so fixated on the past and his own selfish ambition. Knowing he would probably never experience authentic relationships, happiness, and self-love broke my heart for him.

Although I had lived a tortured life with him, he was still the father of my child. Whether that side of him was genuine or not, I wish he has the opportunity to live a fulfilled life.

People think a divorce has to include malice or hate, but I didn't view it that way. Mark had been a part of my life for over 20 years, so I couldn't hate him. Even though the majority of our time together was bad, there were still pockets of goodness sprinkled here and there like the birth of our child.

Truthfully, I knew he would never change. I knew he would never stop until he felt he had won by crushing me, but the thing is, I had already won. I was a victor because I found me, and there was no better reward than that.

21

IT AIN'T OVER-TILL IT'S OVER

I danced around the kitchen listening to Ledisi as I prepared dinner for one. Steak medium well, paired with a 12 oz Maine lobster tail. I was now living for me. Life was different but definitely sweeter.

"Oh no!" I exclaimed when I glanced up at the clock on the wall and saw the time. There were only eight minutes left before the girls and I convened for our monthly FaceTime date.

"Mom!" Nathan called out as he unexpectedly entered the front door. He liked stopping by frequently to check in on me.

"In the kitchen!" I responded.

Nathan appeared in the kitchen with a smile on his face as usual. He kissed me on the cheek quickly and made a beeline for the fridge. "What are you making? It smells amazing" he asked while rummaging through the fridge.

"Surf and turf. But there's only enough for one so..."

"Come on, mom. You and I both know that's not true," he laughed.

I rolled my eyes and couldn't help but giggle. However, I really was preparing a dinner for one. Although Zack and I were beautifully progressing in our relationship, I thought it was only healthy to enjoy alone time.

"Mom, that steak is big enough for two. No way you can eat all of that. You're lucky I'm in a rush. I was in the neighborhood so I thought I'd swing by to check on you. I'll be back later to get what you don't finish," Nathan chuckled as he hurriedly left.

I saw him out and made sure to lock the door behind him. Call it paranoia, but I could have sworn someone had followed me home from the grocery store. It was an uncomfortable feeling that had me looking over my shoulder every few minutes. However, I refused to let anything steal my peace so I shrugged it off.

After plating my food, I sat down to a glass of Pinot noir, lighted candles, my laptop and faint sounds of Ledisi in the background. I opened my laptop just in time for our meeting.

"Hey sistas!" Raquel waved excitedly.

I lit up with a huge smile.

"Mmmmm, Charlie is glowing," Bianca grinned mischievously while leaning in with a wine glass in her hand.

"I see Zack must be doing all the right things," Anthony added.

"What if she's just on like a deep spiritual journey?" Crystal chimed in. "I mean, ever since I found out I was part Native American, I feel the need to connect with my ancestors."

"Girl, you're tripping," Anthony snickered. "What have you been smoking?"

"I'm not kidding," Crystal replied cheekily.

"Babe, you're African American. Embrace it!"

"Whatever, Anthony. I know my roots."

We continued laughing and catching up on their lives while having dinner. It was just like old times. I missed this. I missed our Sunday brunches, trail rides, and nights out on the town.

"This just won't do," Raquel said, interrupting Crystal's riveting story about the man she was seeing.

"What do you mean?" Bianca asked her.

"We need a girl's trip. Let's go to Vegas!"

"I swear all you bitches are high on something today," Anthony sighed.

"I'm serious Anthony. We haven't seen each other in months."

All of a sudden, I heard the sound of glass shattering from the front of the house. I looked around thinking my new puppy, the boys gifted me for Christmas, broke something. They purchased a Dog Argentino with the intention I would have added protection in the house, once she matured in age and size, since I lived alone.

"What was that?" Raquel asked. "Are you okay?"

I pulled out my stun gun hidden in the ornamental fruit bowl and went to inspect the source of the sound. My heart raced as I crouched and peered around the living room wall into the foyer. I began to tremble when I saw shards of glass all over the floor from a broken window.

Next to the broken glass stood my puppy, Ava. I scooped her up in my arms and inspected her for any cuts, which I found none. As I walked back to the living room to get my phone I left on the sofa, Ava began shaking and foaming at the mouth.

"What's going on Charlie?" Raquel sounded from my laptop at the dining room table.

I tried to compose myself but I was too rattled.

"Ss-someone threw a brick through my window and now Ava is shaking and foaming at the mouth like she's been poisoned." There I was frantically fumbling for my phone in the dark so I could call animal poison control.

"I'm calling Nathan," Bianca said, with her phone already in her hand. "I'll tell him to call 911 immediately."

Crystal was also on her phone, but she didn't disclose what she was doing. Instead, she said, "Who would do something so cruel?"

Only one person hated me enough to do anything cruel, but I didn't want to say his name. Besides, I didn't think he was evil enough to fly across the country to torment me, but I could be wrong.

There had been news about robberies going on, but it was nowhere near my home. Of course, I was not naïve to believe it couldn't happen to me, but my gut told me this wasn't a break-in; someone was trying to harm me.

"Oh my God!" Crystal exclaimed. "Charlie... Mark is in LA."

AFTERWORD

Mental abuse is real, and it is silent. From childhood, I believed abuse was only physical, and that blinded me from recognizing the abuse I was subjected to. This is the case for many people.

Healing is an ongoing process. A journey I am happy to be on. My only regret is not leaving sooner. However, if I had to do it all over again I would because I'm at a great place in life spiritually, mentally, physically and financially. I'm more connected to my spirituality than ever before and it is a wonderful feeling. I know without a shadow of a doubt there was divine intervention in my situation. The way things fell into place one after the other to create a way out for me, even to this day, is astounding. It's the evidence of God in my life, and I will forever be grateful.

Zack and I are still seeing each other. Our relationship is beyond healthy and we are taking it one day at a time. We have not defined our relationship yet because I'm not ready for that. I take joy in our freely choosing to love each other every day without being bound to a title or legal agreement. I gave my authentic self to someone for 25 years and in turn I was abused.

Mark has not made a mortgage payment on the house that is in my name in almost two years, although he resides in the home. The loan is now over $60K past due and he refuses to pay, sell and/or move. Therefore, further abusing me financially. He has also been running an ongoing smear campaign against me in the form of a social media platform. He creates video in which he claims I am a narcissist and presents himself as a life coach for NPD survivors. Sadly, he has amassed a following of survivors genuinely looking for help, and these unsuspecting individuals have fallen prey to his manipulation.

I have realized while it's easier to blame the abuser, deflection prevents the healing process. We have to find out what it is within ourselves that draw such people to us and focus on changing to attract more positive connections.

Above all, I hope my journey opens doors of healing for you. Take back control of your mind, your finances, and your life. And may you love yourself enough to put yourself first.

Below are a list of resources you may contact if you are experiencing abuse in any shape or form, feel desperate and not know where to begin. I am here to tell you your feelings are valid and you are not alone.

National Suicide Prevention Lifeline
    800-273-8255
    National Domestic Violence Hotline
    1-800-799-7233
    National Teen dating Abuse Helpline
    1-866-331-9474
    Victim Connect Financial Assistance
    1-855-484-2846

I AM NOT A VICTIM. I AM A SURVIVOR.

ACKNOWLEDGMENTS

Thank you divine spirit of the universe for providing your armor of protection over me and inserting people in my life that helped guide me through unforeseeable times.

I'm forever grateful for the blessing of my sons and their continued love and support.

To my sister, we have been through thick and thin. Thanks for being my protector and confidant. I love you immensely.

And to that special person in my life, thank you for loving me without conditions and encouraging me to always shoot for the moon because as you say "mediocracy is not an option."

I would like to thank my sister-circle for adjusting my crown and encouraging my intellectual, emotional and spiritual growth so I could step into my divine purpose. Pinky promises forever!

My sincere thanks to Faith Musonda for helping me navigate the literary process.

Finally, I am grateful for all the readers and appreciate each and every one of you.

Thanks for reading "Charlie's Secret."

ABOUT THE AUTHOR

Melody Law is a Washington, DC native and proud mother of two. She now resides in sunny Southern California. Melody attended the University of the District of Columbia where she obtained a Bachelor's Degree in Psychology. She is a member of the National Coalition Against Domestic Violence (NCADC), National Organization for Victim Assistance (NOVA), California Partnership to End Domestic Violence (CPEDV) and American Quarter Horse Association (AQHA). In 2016 she co-founded Urban Cowgirls, LLC for the purpose of equine education and emotional therapy. Her favorite pastimes are horseback riding, hiking, gardening, cooking, reading, writing and home renovation projects. She loves hearing from her readers and grateful for every review.

If you'd like to learn more about the author, you can follow her on the social media platforms listed below. You can also email her @melody.a.law@gmail.com

f facebook.com/MelodyLaw

⊙ instagram.com/melody_a_law

Made in the USA
Middletown, DE
25 March 2021